Charles E. Michaels
Lombard Ill.

charles Michaels

TOM HAD THE CAMERA GOING AGAIN NOW.—*Page* 197.
Tom Swift and His Wizard Camera.

TOM SWIFT AND HIS WIZARD CAMERA

OR

Thrilling Adventures While Taking Moving Pictures

BY

VICTOR APPLETON

AUTHOR OF "TOM SWIFT AND HIS MOTOR-CYCLE," "TOM SWIFT AND HIS
SUBMARINE BOAT," "TOM SWIFT AND HIS AIRSHIP,"
"TOM SWIFT AND HIS ELECTRIC RIFLE,"
"TOM SWIFT IN CAPTIVITY," ETC.

ILLUSTRATED

NEW YORK
GROSSET & DUNLAP
PUBLISHERS

COPYRIGHT, 1912 BY
GROSSET & DUNLAP

Tom Swift and His Wizard Camera

CONTENTS

TOM SWIFT AND HIS WIZARD CAMERA

CHAPTER I

A STRANGE OFFER

"SOME one to see you, Mr. Tom."

It was Koku, or August, as he was sometimes called, the new giant servant of Tom Swift, who made this announcement to the young inventor.

"Who is it, Koku?" inquired Tom, looking up from his work-bench in the machine shop, where he was busy over a part of the motor for his new noiseless airship. "Any one I know? Is it the 'Blessing Man?' " for so Koku had come to call Mr. Damon, an eccentric friend of Tom's.

"No, not him. A strange man. I never see before. He say he got quick business."

"Quick business; eh? I guess you mean important, Koku," for this gigantic man, one of a pair that Tom had brought with him after his captivity in "Giant Land," as he called it, could not speak English very well, as yet. "Important business; eh, Koku? Did he send in his card?"

"No, Mr. Tom. Him say he have no card. You not know him, but he very much what you call—recited."

"Excited I guess you mean, Koku. Well, tell him to wait a few minutes, and I'll see him. You can show him in then. But I say, Koku," and Tom paused as he looked at the big man, who had attached himself to our hero, as a sort of personal helper and bodyguard.

"Yes, Mr. Tom; what is it?"

"Don't let him go poking around the shop. He might look at some of my machines that I haven't got fully patented yet. Is he in the front office?"

"That's where him am. He be lookin' at pictures on the walls."

"Oh, that's all right then. Just keep him there. And, Koku, don't let him come back in the shop here, until I get ready to see him. I'll ring the bell when I am."

"All right, Mr. Tom."

Koku, very proud of his mission of keeping guard over the strange visitor, marched from the room with his big strides, his long arms and powerful hands swinging at his sides, for Koku, or August, as Tom had rechristened him, and as he often called him (for it was in the month of August that he had located the giants) was a very powerful man. A veritable giant, being extremely tall, and big in proportion.

"Be sure. Don't let him in here, Koku!" called Tom, in an additional warning, as his new servant left the main shop.

"Sure not!" exclaimed Koku, very earnestly.

"I don't know who he may be," mused Tom, as he began putting away the parts to his new noiseless motor, so that the stranger could not see them, and profit thereby. "It looks rather funny, not sending in his name. It may be some one who thinks he can spring a trick on me, and get some points about my inventions, or dad's.

"It may even be somebody sent on by Andy Foger, or his father. I can't be too careful. I'll just put everything away that isn't fully covered by patents, and then if he wants to infringe on any of the machines I can sue him."

Tom looked about the shop, which was filled with strange machinery, most of which had been made by himself, or his father, or under their combined directions. There was a big biplane in one corner, a small monoplane in another, parts of a submarine boat hanging up overhead, and a small, but very powerful, electric auto waiting to have some repairs made to it, for on his last trip in it Tom Swift had suffered a slight accident.

"There, I guess he can't see anything but what I want him to," mused Tom, as he put away the last part of a new kind of motor, from which he hoped great things. "Let's see, yes, it's out of sight now. I wish Ned Newton, or Mr. Damon were here to be a witness in case he starts anything. But then I have Koku, even if he doesn't speak much English yet. If it comes to blows—well, I wouldn't want that giant to hit *me*," finished Tom with a laugh, as he rang the bell to announce to his servant that the visitor might be shown in.

There was a sound outside the door that separated the business office from the main shop, and Tom heard Koku exclaim:

"Hold on! Wait! I go first. You wait!"

"What's the matter with *me* going ahead?" demanded a quick, snappy voice. "I'm in a hurry, and——"

"You wait! I go first," was the giant's reply, "and then came the sound of a scuffle.

"Ouch! Say! Hold on there, my man! Take your hand off my shoulder! You're crushing me with those big fingers of yours!"

This was evidently the visitor remonstrating with the giant.

"Humph! I guess Koku must have grabbed him," said Tom softly. "I don't like that sort of a visitor. What's his hurry getting in here?" and our hero looked about, to see if he had a weapon at hand in case of an attack. Often cranks had forced their way into his shop, with pet inventions which they wanted him to perfect after they had themselves failed. Tom saw a heavy iron bar at hand, and knew this would serve to protect him.

"You come after me!" exclaimed Koku, when the voice of the other had ceased. "Do you stand under me?"

"Oh, yes, I understand all right. I'll keep back. But I didn't mean anything. I'm just in a hurry to see Tom Swift, that is all. I'm always in a hurry in fact. I've lost nearly a thousand dollars this morning, just by this delay. I want to see Mr. Swift at once; and have a talk with him."

"Another crank, I guess," mused Tom. "Well, I'm not going to waste much time on him."

A moment later the door opened, and into the shop stepped Koku, followed by a short, stout, fussy little man, wearing a flaming red tie, but otherwise his clothes were not remarkable.

"Is this Mr. Tom Swift?" asked the stranger,

as he advanced and held out his hand to the young man.

"Yes," answered Tom, looking carefully at the visitor. He did not seem to be dangerous, he had no weapon, and, Tom was relieved to note that he did not carry some absurd machine, or appliance, that he had made, hoping to get help in completing it. The youth was trying to remember if he had ever seen the stranger before, but came to the conclusion that he had not.

"Sorry to take up your time," went on the man, "but I just *had* to see you. No one else will do. I've heard lots about you. That was a great stunt you pulled off, getting those giants for the circus. This is one; isn't he?" and he nodded toward Koku.

"Yes," replied Tom, wondering if the little man was in such a hurry why he did not get down to business.

"I thought so," the caller went on, as he shook hands with Tom. "Once you felt his grip you'd know he was a giant, even if you didn't see him. Yes, that was a great stunt. And going to the caves of ice, too, and that diamond-making affair. All of 'em great. I——"

"How did you know about them?" interrupted Tom, wishing the man would tell his errand.

"Oh, you're better known than you have any

idea of, Tom Swift. As soon as I got this idea
of mine I said right away, to some of the others
in my business, I says, says I, 'Tom Swift is the
boy for us. I'll get him to undertake this work,
and then it will be done to the Queen's taste.
Tom's the boy who can do it,' I says, and they all
agreed with me. So I came here to-day, and I'm
sorry I had to wait to see you, for I'm the busiest
man in the world, I believe, and, as I said, I've
lost about a thousand dollars waiting to have a
talk with you. I——"

"I am sorry," interrupted Tom, and he was not
very cordial. "But I was busy, and——"

"All right! All right! Don't apologize!" broke
in the man in rapid tones, while both Tom, and
his servant, Koku, looked in surprise at the quick
flow of language that came from him. "Don't
apologize for the world. It's my fault for both-
ering you. And I'll lose several thousand dollars,
willingly, if you'll undertake this job. I'll make
money from it as it is. It's worth ten thousand
dollars to you, I should say, and I'm willing to
pay that."

He looked about, as though for a seat, and
Tom, apologizing for his neglect in offering one,
shoved a box forward.

"We don't have chairs in here," said the

young inventor with a smile. "Now if you will tell me what you——"

"I'm coming right to it. I'll get down to business in a moment," interrupted the man as he sat down on the box, not without a grunt or two, for he was very stout. "I'm going to introduce myself in just a second, and then I'm going to tell you who I am. And I hope you'll take up my offer, though it may seem a strange one."

The man took out a pocketbook, and began searching through it, evidently for some card or paper.

"He's as odd as Mr. Damon is, when he's blessing everything," mused Tom, as he watched the man.

"I thought I had a card with me, but I haven't," the visitor went on. "No matter. I'm James Period—promoter of all kinds of amusement enterprises, from a merry-go-'round to a theatrical performance. I want you to——"

"No more going after giants," interrupted Tom. "It's too dangerous, and I haven't time to——"

"No, it has nothing to do with giants," spoke Mr. Period, as he glanced up at Koku, who towered over him as he sat on the box near Tom.

"Well?" returned Tom.

"This is something entirely new. It has never been done before, though if you *should* happen to be able to get a picture of giants don't miss the opportunity."

"Get a *picture?*" exclaimed Tom, wondering if, after all, his visitor might not be a little insane.

"Pictures, yes. Listen. I'm James Period. Jim, if you like it better, or just plain 'Spotty.' That's what most of my friends call me. Get the idea? A period is a spot. I'm a Period, therefor I'm a spot. But that isn't the real reason. It's because I'm always Johnny on the Spot when anything is happening. If it's a big boxing exhibition, I'm there. If it's a coronation, I'm there, or some of my men are. If it's a Durbar in India, you'll find Spotty on the spot. That's me. If there's going to be a building blown up with dynamite—I'm on hand; or some of my men. If there's a fire I get there as soon as the engines do—if it's a big one. Always on the spot—that's me—James Period—Spotty for short. Do you get me?" and he drew a long breath and looked at Tom, his head on one side.

"I understand that you are——"

"In the moving picture business," interrupted Mr. Period, who never seemed to let Tom finish a sentence. "I'm the biggest moving picture man in the world—not in size, but in business. I make all the best films. You've seen some of 'em I guess. Every one of 'em has my picture on the end of the film. Shows up great. Advertising scheme—get me?"

"Yes," replied Tom, as he recalled that he had seen some of the films in question, and good ones they were too. "I see your point, but——"

"You want to know why I come to you; don't you?" again interrupted "Spotty," with a laugh. "Well, I'll tell you. I need you in my business. I want you to invent a new kind of moving picture camera. A small light one—worked by electricity—a regular wizard camera. I want you to take it up in an airship with you, and then go to all sorts of wild and strange countries, Africa, India—the jungles—get pictures of wild animals at peace and fighting—herds of elephants—get scenes of native wars—earthquakes—eruptions of volcanoes—all the newest and most wonderful pictures you can. You'll have to make a new kind of camera to do it. The kind we use won't do the trick.

"Now do you get me? I'm going to give you ten thousand dollars, above all your expenses, for some films such as I've been speaking of. I want novelty. Got to have it in my business! You can do it. Now will you?"

"I hardly think——" began Tom.

"Don't answer me now," broke in Mr. Period.
"Take four minutes to think it over. Or even
five. I guess I can wait that long. Take five
minutes. I'll wait while you make up your mind,
but I know you'll do it. Five minutes—no more,"
and hastily getting up off the box Mr. Period
began impatiently pacing up and down the shop.

Jackson, an engineer employed by the Swifts. These were all the immediate members of the household.

Tom had a chum, Ned Newton, who used to work in a bank, and there was a girl, Mary Nestor, a daughter of Amos Nestor, in which young lady Tom was much interested.

Eradicate Sampson had a mule, Boomerang, of whom he thought almost as much as he did of Tom. Eradicate was a faithful friend and servant, but, of late, Koku, or August, the giant, had rather supplanted him. I must not forget Mr. Wakefield Damon, of Waterfield, a village near Shopton. Mr. Damon was an odd man, always blessing everything. He and Tom were good friends, and had been on many trips together.

The first book of the series was called "Tom Swift and His Motor-Cycle," and related how Tom bought the cycle from Mr. Damon, after the latter had met with an accident on it, and it was in this way that our hero became acquainted with the odd man.

Tom had many adventures on his motor-cycle, and, later on he secured a motor-boat, in which he beat his enemy, Andy Foger, in a race. Next Tom built an airship, and in this he went on a wonderful trip. Returning from this he and his father heard about a treasure sunken under the ocean. In his submarine boat Tom secured the valuables, and made a large sum for himself.

In his electric runabout, which was the swiftest car on the road, Tom was able to save from ruin a bank in which his father was interested, and, a short time after that, he went on a trip in an airship, with a man who had invented a new kind. The airship was smashed, and fell to Earthquake Island, where there were some refugees from a shipwreck, among them being the parents of Mary Nestor. In the volume called "Tom Swift and His Wireless Message," I told how he saved these people.

When Tom went among the diamond makers he had more strange adventures, on that trip discovering the secret of phantom mountain. He had bad luck when he went to the caves of ice, for there his airship was wrecked.

When Tom made the trip in his sky racer he broke all records for an aerial flight, incidentally saving his father's life. It was some time after this when he invented an electric rifle, and went to elephant land, to rescue some missionaries from the red pygmies.

The eleventh volume of the series is called "Tom Swift in the Land of Gold," and relates his adventures underground, while the next one

tells of a new machine he invented—an air-glider
—which he used to save the exiles of Siberia, incidentally, on that trip, finding a valuable de-
posit of platinum.

As I have said, it was on his trip to giant
land that Tom got his big servant. This book,
the thirteenth of the series, is called "Tom Swift
in Captivity," for the giants captured him and
his friends, and it was only by means of their
airship that they made their daring escape.

Tom had been back from the strange land
some time now. One giant he had turned over
to the circus representative for whom he had
undertaken the mission, and the other he re-
tained to work around his shop, as Eradicate was
getting too old. It was now winter, and there
had been quite a fall of snow the day before
Mr. Period, the odd moving picture man, called
on Tom. There were many big drifts outside
the building.

Tom had fitted up a well-equipped shop, where
he and his father worked on their inventions.
Occasionally Ned Newton, or Mr. Damon, would
come over to help them, but of late Tom had
been so busy on his noiseless motor that he had
not had time to even see his friends.

"Well, I guess the five minutes have passed,
and my mind is made up," thought Tom, as he

looked at his watch. "I might as well tell Mr. Period that I can't undertake his commission. In the first place it isn't going to be an easy matter to make an electric moving picture camera. I'd have to spend a lot of time studying up the subject, and then I might not be able to get it to work right.

"And, again, I can't spare the time to go to all sorts of wild and impossible places to get the pictures. It's all well enough to talk about getting moving pictures of natives in battle, or wild beasts fighting, or volcanoes in action, but it isn't so easy to do it. Then, too, I'd have to make some changes in my airship if I went on that trip. No, I can't go. I'll tell him he'll have to find some one else."

Mr. Period pulled out his watch, opened it quickly, snapped it shut again, and exclaimed:

"Well, how about it, Tom Swift? When can you start! The sooner the better for me! You'll want some money for expenses I think. I brought my check book along, also a fountain pen. I'll give you a thousand dollars now, for I know making an electric moving picture camera isn't going to be cheap work. Then, when you get ready to start off in your airship, you'll need more money. I'll be Johnny-on-the-spot all right, and have it ready for you.   Now when do you think you can start?"

He sat down at a bench, and began filling out a check.

"Hold on!" cried Tom, amused in spite of himself.   "Don't sign that check, Mr. Period.   I'm not going."

"Not going?"   The man's face showed blank amazement.

"No," went on Tom.   "I can't spare the time. I'm sorry, but you'll have to get some one else."

"Some one else?   But who can I get?"

"Why, there are plenty who would be glad of the chance."

"But they can't invent an electric moving picture camera, and, if they could, they wouldn't know enough to take pictures with it.   It's got to be you or no one, Tom Swift.   Look here, I'll make it fifteen thousand dollars above expenses."

"No, I'm sorry, but I can't go.   My work here keeps me too busy."

"Oh, pshaw!   Now, look here, Tom Swift! Do you know who sent me to see you?"

"No."

"It was Mr. Nestor, who has a daughter named Mary, I believe.   Mr. Nestor is one of the directors in our company, and one day, when he told me about you sending a wireless message from Earthquake Island, I knew you would be the very man for me. So now you see you'll be doing Mr. Nestor a favor, as well as me, if you go on this trip."

Tom was somewhat surprised, yet he realized that Mr. Period was speaking the truth. Mr. Nestor was identified with many new enterprises. Yet the youth was firm.

"I really can't go," said our hero. "I'd like to, but I can't. I'd like to oblige Mr. Nestor, for —well, for more reasons than one," and Tom blushed slightly. "But it is out of the question. I really can't go."

"But you *must!*" insisted the camera man. "I won't take 'no' for an answer. You've got to go, Tom Swift, do you hear that? You've *got* to go?"

Mr. Period was apparently very much excited. He strode over to ,Tom, and smote his hands together to emphasize what he said. Then he shook his finger at Tom, to impress the importance of the matter on our hero.

"You've just *got* to go!" he cried. "You're the only one who can help me, Tom. Do go! I'll pay you well, and—oh, well, I know you don't need the money, exactly, but—say, you've got to go!"

In his earnestness Mr. Period laid his hand on Tom's arm. The next instant something happened.

With a few big strides Koku was beside the picture man. With great quickness he grasped Mr. Period by the coat collar, lifted him off his feet with one hand, and walked over to a window with him, easily lifting him above the floor.

With one fling the giant tossed the short, stout gentleman out into a snow bank, while Tom looked on, too surprised to do anything, even if he had had the chance.

"There. You touch Tom Swift again, and I sit on you and keep you under snow!" cried the giant, while Mr. Period kicked and squirmed about in the drift, as Tom made a leap forward to help him out.

CHAPTER III

TOM MAKES UP HIS MIND

"GREAT SCOTT!" yelled the picture man. "What in the world happened to me? Did I get kicked by that mule Boomerang of Eradicate's, that I've heard so much about? Or was it an earthquake, such as I want to get a picture of? What happened?"

He was still floundering about in the deep bank of snow that was just outside the window. Fortunately the sash had been up, and Koku had tossed Mr. Period through the open window. Otherwise, had there been glass, the well-meaning, but unreasoning giant would probably have thrown his victim through that, and he might have been badly cut. Tom had the window open for fresh air, as it was rather close in the shop.

"Why, Koku!" exclaimed the young inventor, as he leaned out of the window, and extended his hand to the moving picture man to help him out of the drift. "What do vou mean by that?" Have you gone crazy?"

"No, but no one shall lay hands on my master!" declared the giant half savagely. "I have vowed to always protect you from danger, in return for what you did for me. I saw this man lay his hand on you. In another moment he might have killed you, had not Koku been here. There is no danger when I am by," and he stretched out his huge arms, and looked ferocious. "I have turned over that man, your enemy!" he added.

"Yes, you overturned me all right," admitted Mr. Period, as he got to his feet, and crawled in through the window to the shop again. "I went head over heels. I'm glad it was clean snow, and not a mud bank, Tom. What in the world is the matter with him?"

"I guess he thought you were going to harm me," said Tom in a low voice, as the picture man came in the shop. "Koku is very devoted to me, and sometimes he makes trouble," the youth went on. "But he means it all for the best. I am very sorry for what happened," and Tom aided Mr. Period in brushing the snow off his garments. "Koku, you must beg the pardon of this gentleman," Tom directed.

"What for?" the giant wanted to know.

"For throwing him into the snow. It is not allowed to do such things in this country, even though it is in Giant Land. Beg his pardon."

"I shall not," said the giant calmly, for Tom
had taught him to speak fairly good English,
though sometimes he got his words backwards.
"The man was about to kill you, and I stopped
him—I will stop him once more, though if he
does not like the snow, I can throw him somewhere else."

"No! No! You must not do it!" cried Tom.
"He meant no harm. He is my friend."

"I am glad to hear you say that," exclaimed
the picture man. "I have hopes that you will do
what I want."

"He your friend?" asked Koku wonderingly.

"Certainly; and you must beg his pardon for
what you did," insisted Tom.

"Very well. I am glad you did not hurt yourself," said the giant, and with that "apology" he
stalked out of the room, his feelings evidently
very much disturbed.

"Ha! Ha!" laughed Mr. Period. "I guess
he can't see any one but you, Tom. But never
mind. I know he didn't mean anything, and, as
I'm none the worse I'll forgive him. My necktie
isn't spotted; is it?"

"No, the snow didn't seem to do that any
harm," replied the young inventor, as he looked
at the brilliant piece of red silk around Mr. Period's collar.

"I am very particular about my neckties," went on the picture man. "I always wear one color. My friends never forget me then."

Tom wondered how they could ever forget him, even though he wore no tie, for his figure and face were such as to not easily be forgotten.

"I'm glad it's not soiled," went on "Spotty" as he liked to be called. "Now, Tom, you said you were my friend. Prove it by accepting my offer. Build that wizard camera, and get me some moving pictures that will be a sensation. Say you will!"

He looked appealingly at Tom, and, remembering the rather rude and unexpected treatment to which Koku had submitted the gentleman, Tom felt his mind changing. Still he was not yet ready to give in. He rather liked the idea the more he thought of it, but he felt that he had other duties, and much to occupy him at home, especially if he perfected his silent motor.

"Will you go?" asked Mr. Period, picking up his fountain pen and check book, that he had laid aside when he walked over to Tom, just before the giant grasped him. "Say you will."

The young inventor was silent a moment. He thought over the many adventures he had gone through—in the caves of ice, in the city of gold, escaping from the giants, and the red pygmies—

he went over the details of his trips through the air, of the dangers under the seas, of those he had escaped from on Earthquake Island. Surely he was entitled to a little rest at home.

And yet there was a lure to it all. A certain fascination that was hard to resist. Mr. Period must have seen what was going on in Tom's mind, for he said:

"I know you're going. I can see it. Why, it will be just the very thing you need. You'll get more fame out of this thing than from any of your other inventions. Come, say you'll do it.

"I'll tell you what I'll do!" he went on eagerly. "After you make the camera, and take a lot of films, showing strange and wonderful scenes, I'll put at the end of each film, next to my picture, your name, and a statement showing that you took the originals. How's that? Talk about being advertised! Why you can't beat it! Millions of people will read your name at the picture shows every night."

"I am not looking for advertisements," said Tom, with a laugh.

"Well, then, think of the benefit you will be to science," went on Mr. Period quickly. "Think of the few people who have seen wild animals as they are, of those who have ever seen an earthquake, or a volcano in action. You can go to

Japan, and get pictures of earthquakes. They have them on tap there. And as for volcanoes, why the Andes mountains are full of 'em. Think of how many people will be thankful to you for showing them these wonderful scenes."

"And think of what might happen if I should take a tumble into a crack in the earth, or down a hot volcano, or fall into a jungle when there was a fight on among the elephants," suggested Tom. "My airship might take a notion to go down when I was doing the photographing," he added.

"No. Nothing like that will happen to Tom Swift," was the confident answer of the picture man. "I've read of your doings. You don't have accidents that you can't get the better of. But come, I know you're thinking of it, and I'm sure you'll go. Let me make you out this check, sign a contract which I have all ready, and then get to work on the camera."

Tom was silent a moment. Then he said:

"Well, I admit that there is something attractive about it. I hoped I was going to stay home for a long time. But——"

"Then you'll go!" cried Mr. Period eagerly. "Here's the money," and he quickly filled out a check for Tom's first expenses, holding the slip of paper toward the young inventor.

"Wait a minute! Hold on!" cried Tom. "Not so fast if you please. I haven't yet made up my mind."

"But you will; won't you?" asked Mr. Period.

"Well, I'll make up my mind, one way or the other," replied the young man. "I won't say I'll go, but——"

"I'll tell you what I'll do!" interrupted Mr. Period. "I'm a busy man, and every second is worth money to me. But I'll wait for you to make up your mind. I'll give you until to-morrow night. How's that? Fair, isn't it?"

"Yes, I think so. I am afraid——"

"I'm not!" broke in the picture man. "I know you'll decide to go. Think of the fun and excitement you'll have. Now I've taken up a lot of your time, and I'm going to leave you alone. I'll be back to-morrow evening for my answer. But I know you're going to get those moving pictures for me. Is that giant of yours anywhere about?" he asked, as he looked cautiously around before leaving the shop. "I don't want to fall into his hands again."

"I don't blame you," agreed Tom. "I never knew him to act that way before. But I'll go to the gate with you, and Koku will behave himself. I am sorry——"

"Don't mention it!" broke in the picture man.

"It was worth all I suffered, if you go, and I
know you will. Don't trouble yourself to come
out. I can find my way, and if your giant comes
after me, I'll call for help."

He hurried out before Tom could follow, and,
hearing the gate click a little later, and no call for
help coming, our hero concluded that his visitor
had gotten safely away.

"Well, what am I going to do about it?"
mused Tom, as he resumed work on his silent
motor. He had not been long engaged in re-
adjusting some of the valves, when he was again
interrupted.

This time it was his chum, Ned Newton, who
entered, and, as Ned was well known to the
giant, nothing happened.

"Well, what's up, Tom?" asked Ned.

"Why, did you notice anything unusual?"
asked Tom.

"I saw Koku standing at the gate a while ago,
looking down the road at a short stout man, with
a red tie. Your giant seemed rather excited
about something."

"Oh, yes. I'll tell you about it," and Tom
related the details of Mr. Period's visit.

"Are you going to take his offer?" asked Ned.

"I've got until to-morrow to make up my
mind. What would you do, Ned?"

"Why, I'd take it in a minute, if I knew how to make an electric camera. I suppose it has to be a very speedy one, to take the kind of pictures he wants. Wait, hold on, I've just thought of a joke. It must be a swift camera—catch on—you're Swift, and you make a swift camera; see the point?"

"I do," confessed Tom, with a laugh. "Well, Ned, I've been thinking it over, but I can't decide right away. I will to-morrow night, though."

"Then I'm coming over, and hear what it is. If you decide to go, maybe you'll take me along."

"I certainly will, and Mr. Damon, too."

"How about the giant?"

"Well, I guess there'll be room for him. But I haven't decided yet. Hand me that wrench over there; will you," and then Tom and Ned began talking about the new apparatus on which the young inventor was working.

True to his promise Mr. Period called the next evening. He found Tom, Ned and Mr. Swift in the library, talking over various matters.

"Well, Tom, have you made up your mind?" asked the caller, when Mrs. Baggert, the housekeeper, had shown him into the room. "I hope you have, and I hope it is favorable to me."

"Yes," said Tom slowly, "I've thought it all over, and I have decided that I will——"

At that moment there was a loud shouting outside the house, and the sound of some one running rapidly through the garden that was just outside the low library window—a garden now buried deep under snow.

"What's that?" cried Ned, jumping to his feet.

"That was Koku's voice," replied Tom, "and I guess he was chasing after some one."

"They'll need help if that giant gets hold of them," spoke Mr. Period solemnly, while the noise outside increased in volume.

CHAPTER IV

HELD FAST

"Here, Tom! Come back! Where are you going?" cried aged Mr. Swift, as his son started toward the window.

"I'm going to see what's up, and who it is that Koku is chasing," replied the young inventor.

As he spoke he opened the window, which went all the way down to the floor. He stepped out on a small balcony, put his hand on the railing, and was about to leap over. Back of him was his father, Mr. Period and Ned.

"Come back! You may get hurt!" urged Mr. Swift. He had aged rapidly in the last few months, and had been obliged to give up most of his inventive work. Naturally, he was very nervous about his son.

"Don't worry, dad; replied the youth. "I'm not in much danger when Koku is around."

"That's right, agreed the moving picture man. "I'd sooner have that giant look after me than half a dozen policemen."

31

"Only jes' had a glimpse ob his back."

"Well, you go back to the house and tell father and Mr. Period about it. Ned and I will go on with Koku. I hope to get the fellow."

"Why, Tom?" asked his chum.

"Because I think he was after bigger game than chickens. My noiseless motor, for the new airship, is nearly complete, and it may have been some one trying to get that. I received an offer from a concern the other day, who wished to purchase it, and, when I refused to sell, they seemed rather put out."

The two lads raced on, while Eradicate tottered back to the house, where he found Mr. Swift and the picture man awaiting him.

"I guess he got away," remarked Ned, after he and his chum had covered nearly the length of the big garden.

"I'm afraid so," agreed Tom. "I can't hear Koku any more. Still, I'm not going to give up."

Pantingly they ran on, and, a little later, they met the big man coming back.

"Did he get away?" asked Tom.

"Yes, Mr. Tom, he scaped me all right."

"*Escaped* you mean, Koku. Well, never mind. You did your best."

"I would like to have hold of him," spoke the giant, as he stretched out his big arms.

"Did you know who he was?" inquired Ned.

"No, I couldn't see his face," and he gave the same description of the affair as had Eradicate.

"Was it a full grown man, or some one about my size?" Tom wanted to know.

"A man," replied the giant.

"Why do you ask that?" inquired Ned, as the big fellow went on to resume his talk with Eradicate, and the two chums turned to go into the house, after the fruitless chase.

"Because, I thought it might be Andy Foger," was Tom's reply. "It would be just like him, but if it was a *man,* it couldn't be him. Andy's rather short."

"Besides, he doesn't live here any more," said Ned.

"I know, but I heard Sam Snedecker, who used to be pretty thick with him, saying the other day that he expected a visit from Andy. I hope he doesn't come back to Shopton, even for a day, for he always tries to make trouble for me. Well, let's go in, and tell 'em all about our chase after a chicken thief."

"And so he got away?" remarked Mr. Swift, when Tom had completed his story.

"Yes," answered the young inventor, as he closed, and locked, the low library window, for there was a chilly breeze blowing. "I think I will have to rig up the burglar alarm on my shop again. I don't want to take any chances."

"Do you remember what we were talking about, when that interruption came?" asked Mr. Period, after a pause. "You were saying, Tom, that you had made up your mind, and that was as far as you got. What is your answer to my offer?"

"Well," spoke the lad slowly, and with a smile, "I think I will——"

"Now don't say 'no' "; interrupted the picture man. "If you are going to say 'no' take five minutes more, or even ten, and think it over carefully. I want you——"

"I wasn't going to say 'no,' " replied Tom. "I have decided to accept your offer, and I'll get right at work on the electrical camera, and see what I can do in the way of getting moving pictures for you."

"You will? Say, that's great! That's fine! I knew you would accept, but I was the least bit afraid you might not, without more urging."

"Of course," began Tom, "it will take——"

"Not another word. Just wait a minute," interrupted Mr. Period in his breezy fashion. "Take this."

He quickly filled out a check and handed it to Tom.

"Now sign this contract, which merely says that you will do your best to get pictures for me, and that you won't do it for any other concern, and everything will be all right. Sign there," he added, pointing to a dotted line, and thrusting a fountain pen into Tom's hand. The lad read over the agreement, which was fair enough, and signed it, and Ned affixed his name as a witness.

"Now when can you go?" asked Mr. Period eagerly.

"Not before Spring, I'm afraid," replied Tom. "I have first to make the camera, and then my airship needs overhauling if I am to go on such long trips as will be necessary in case I am to get views of wild beasts in the jungle."

"Well, make it as soon as you can," begged Mr. Period. "I can have the films early next Fall then, and they will be in season for the Winter runs at the theatres. Now, I'm the busiest man in the world, and I believe I have lost five hundred dollars by coming here to-night. Still, I don't regret it. I'm going back now, and I'll expect to hear from you when you are ready to start. There's my address. Good-bye," and thrusting a card into Tom's hand he hurried out of the room.

"Won't you stop all night?" called Mr. Swift after him.

"Sorry. I'd like to but can't. Got a big contract I must close in New York to-morrow morning. I've ordered a special train to be at the Shopton station in half an hour, and I must catch that. Good night!" and Mr. Period hurried away.

"Say, he's a hustler all right!" exclaimed Ned.

"Yes, and I've got to hustle if I invent that camera," added Tom. "It's got to be a specially fast one, and one that can take pictures from a long distance. Electricity is the thing to use, I guess."

"Then you are really going off on this trip, Tom?" asked his father, rather wistfully.

"I'm afraid I am," replied his son. "I thought I could stay at home for a while, but it seems not."

"I was in hopes you could give me a little time to help me on my gyroscope invention," went on the aged man. "But I suppose it will keep until you come back. It is nearly finished."

"Yes, and I don't like stopping work on my noiseless motor," spoke Tom. "But that will have to wait, too."

"Do you know where you are going?" inquired Ned.

"Well, I'll have to do considerable traveling I suppose to get all the films he wants. But once

I'm started I'll like it I guess. Of course you're
coming, Ned."

"I hope so."

"Of course you are!" insisted Tom, as if that
settled it. "And I'm sure Mr. Damon will go
also. I haven't seen him in some time. I hope
he isn't ill."

Tom started work on his Wizard Camera, as
he called it, the next day—that is he began draw-
ing the designs, and planning how to construct
it. Ned helped him, and Koku was on hand in
case he was needed, but there was little he could
do, as yet. Tom made an inspection of his shop
the morning after the chicken thief scare, but
nothing seemed to have been disturbed.

A week passed, and Tom had all the plans
drawn for the camera. He had made several
experiments with different forms of electricity
for operating the mechanism, and had decided on
a small, but very powerful, storage battery to
move the film, and take the pictures.

This storage battery, which would be inside the
camera, would operate it automatically. That
is, the camera could be set up any place, in the
jungle, or on the desert, it could be left alone,
and would take pictures without any one being
near it. Tom planned to have it operate at a certain set time, and stop at a certain time, and he

could set the dials to make this time any moment of the day or night. For there was to be a powerful light in connection with the camera, in order that night views might be taken. Be sides being automatic the camera could be worked by hand.

When it was not necessary to have the camera operate by the storage battery, it could be connected to wires and worked by an ordinary set of batteries, or by a dynamo. This was for use on the airship, where there was a big electrical machine. I shall tell you more about the camera as the story proceeds.

One afternoon Tom was alone in the shop, for he had sent Koku on an errand, and Eradicate was off in a distant part of the grounds, doing some whitewashing, which was his specialty. Ned had not come over, and Mr. Swift, having gone to see some friends, and Mrs. Baggert being at the store, Tom, at this particular time, was rather isolated.

He was conducting some delicate electrical experiments, and to keep the measuring instruments steady he had closed all the windows and doors of his shop. The young inventor was working at a bench in one corner, and near him, standing upright, was a heavy shaft of iron, part of his submarine, wrapped in burlap, and padded, to keep it from rusting.

"Now," said Tom to himself, as he mixed two kinds of acid in a jar, to produce a new sort of electrical current, "I will see if this is any better than the first way in which I did it."

He was careful about pouring out the powerful stuff, but, in spite of this, he spilled a drop on his finger. It burned like fire, and, instinctively, he jerked his hand back.

The next instant there was a series of happenings. Tom's elbow came in contact with another jar of acid, knocking it over, and spilling it into the retort where he had been mixing the first two liquids. There was a hissing sound, as the acids combined, and a thick, white vapor arose, puffing into Tom's face, and making him gasp.

He staggered back, brushed against the heavy iron shaft in the corner, and it fell sideways against him, knocking him to the floor, and dropping across his thighs. The padding on it saved him from broken bones, but the shaft was so heavy, that after it was on him, Tom could not move. He was held fast on the floor of his shop, unable to use his legs, and prevented from getting up.

For a moment Tom was stunned, and then he called:

"Help! Help! Eradicate! Koku! Help!"

He waited a moment, but there was only a silence.

And then Tom smelled a strange odor—an odor of a choking gas that seemed to smother him.

It's the acids!" he cried. "They're generating gas! And I'm held fast here! The place is closed up tight, and I can't move! Help! Help!"

But there was no one at hand to aid Tom, and every moment the fumes of the gas became stronger. Desperately the youth struggled to rid himself of the weight of the shaft, but he could not. And then he felt his senses leaving him, for the powerful gas was making him unconscious.

CHAPTER V

TOM GETS A WARNING

"BLESS my shoe buttons!" exclaimed a voice, as a man came toward Tom's shop, a little later. "Bless my very necktie! This is odd. I go to the house, and find no one there. I come out here, and not a soul is about. Tom Swift can't have gone off on another one of his wonderful trips, without sending me word. I know he wouldn't do that. And yet, bless my watch and chain, I can't find any one!"

It was Mr. Damon who spoke, as my old readers have already guessed. He peered into one of the shop windows, and saw something like a fog filling the place.

"That's strange," he went on. "I don't see Tom there, and yet it looks as if an experiment was going on. I wonder——"

Mr. Damon heard some one coming up behind him, and turned to see Koku the giant, who was returning from the errand on which Tom had sent him.

"Oh, Koku, it's you; is it?" the odd man asked. "Bless my cuff buttons! Where is Tom?"

"In shop I guess."

"I don't see him. Still I had better look. There doesn't seem to be any one about."

Mr. Damon opened the shop door, and was met by such an outward rush of choking gas that he staggered back.

"Bless my——" he began but he had to stop, to cough and gasp. "There must have been some sort of an accident," he cried, as he got his lungs full of fresh air. "A bad accident! Tom could never work in that atmosphere. Whew!"

"Accident! What is matter?" cried Koku stepping to the doorway. He, too choked and gasped, but his was such a strong and rugged nature, and his lungs held such a supply of air, that it took more than mere gas to knock him out. He peered in through the wreaths of the acid vapor, and saw the body of his master, lying on the floor—held down by the heavy iron.

In another instant Koku had rushed in, holding his breath, for, now that he was inside the place, the gas made even him feel weak.

"Come back! Come back!" cried Mr. Damon. You'll be smothered! Wait until the gas escapes!"

"Then Mr. Tom die!" cried the giant. "I get him—or I no come out."

With one heave of his powerful right arm, Koku lifted the heavy shaft from Tom's legs. Then, gathering the lad up in his left arm, as if he were a baby, Koku staggered out into the fresh air, almost falling with his burden, as he neared Mr. Damon, for the giant was well-nigh overcome.

"Bless my soul!" cried the odd man. "Is he— is he——"

He did not finish the sentence, but, as Koku laid Tom down on the overcoat of Mr. Damon, which the latter quickly spread on the snow, the eccentric man put his hand over the heart of the young inventor.

"It beats!" he murmured. "He's alive, but very weak. We must get a doctor at once. I'll do what I can. There's no time to spare. Bless my——"

But Mr. Damon concluded that there was no time for blessing anything, and so he stopped short.

"Carry him up to the house, Koku," he said. "I know where there are some medicines, and I'll try to revive him while we're waiting for the doctor. Hurry!"

Tom was laid on a lounge, and, just then, Mrs. Baggert came in.

"Telephone for the doctor!" cried Mr. Damon to the housekeeper, who kept her nerve, and did not get excited. "I'll give Tom some ammonia, and other stimulants, and see if I can bring him around. Koku, get me some cold water."

The telephone was soon carrying the message to the doctor, who promised to come at once. Koku, in spite of his size, was quick, and soon brought the water, into which Mr. Damon put some strong medicine, that he found in a closet. Tom's eyelids fluttered as the others forced some liquid between his lips.

"He's coming around!" cried the eccentric man. "I guess he'll be all right, Koku."

"Koku glad," said the giant simply, for he loved Tom with a deep devotion.

"Yes, Koku, if it hadn't been for you, though, I don't believe that he would be alive. That was powerful gas, and a few seconds more in there might have meant the end of Tom. I didn't see him lying on the floor, until after you rushed in. Bless my thermometer! It is very strange."

They gave Tom more medicine, rubbed his arms and legs, and held ammonia under his nose. Slowly he opened his eyes, and in a faint voice asked:

"Where—am—I?"

"In your own house," replied Mr. Damon, cheerfully. "How do you feel?"

"I'm—all—right—now," said Tom slowly. He felt his strength coming gradually back, and he remembered what had happened, though he did not yet know how he had been saved. The doctor came in at this moment, with a small medical battery, which completed the restorative work begun by the others. Soon Tom could sit up, though he was still weak and rather sick.

"Who brought me out?" he asked, when he had briefly told how the accident occurred.

"Koku did," replied Mr. Damon. "I guess none of the rest of us could have lifted the iron shaft from your legs."

"It's queer how that fell," said Tom, with a puzzled look on his face. "I didn't hit it hard enough to bring it down. Beside, I had it tied to nails, driven into the wall, to prevent just such an accident as this. I must see about it when I get well."

"Not for a couple of days," exclaimed the doctor grimly. "You've got to stay in bed a while yet. You had a narrow escape, Tom Swift."

"Well, I'm glad I went to Giant Land," said the young inventor, with a wan smile. "Otherwise I'd never have Koku," and he looked af-

fectionately at the big man, who laughed happily.
In nature Koku was much like a child.

Mr. Swift came home a little later, and Ned
Newton called, both being very much surprised to
hear of the accident. As for Eradicate, the poor
old colored man was much affected, and would
have sat beside Tom's bed all night, had they
allowed him.

Our hero recovered rapidly, once the fumes
of the gas left his system, and, two days later,
he was able to go out to the shop again. At his
request everything had been left just as it was
after he had been brought out. Of course the
fumes of the gas were soon dissipated, when
the door was opened, and the acids, after
mingling and giving off the vapor, had become
neutralized, so that they were now harmless.

"Now I'm going to see what made that shaft
fall," said Tom to Ned, as the two chums walked
over to the bench where the young inventor had
been working. "The tap I gave it never ought
to have brought it down."

Together they examined the thin, but strong,
cords that had been passed around the shaft,
having been fastened to two nails, driven into
the wall.

"Look!" cried Tom, pointing to one of the
cords.

"What is it?" asked Ned.

"The strands were partly cut through, so that only a little jar was enough to break the remaining ones," went on Tom. "They've been cut with a knife, too, and not frayed by vibration against the nail, as might be the case. Ned, someone has been in my shop, meddling, and he wanted this shaft to fall. This is a trick!"

"Great Scott, Tom! You don't suppose any one wanted that shaft to fall on you; do you?"

"No, I don't believe that. Probably some one wanted to damage the shaft, or he might have thought it would topple over against the bench, and break some of my tools, instruments or machinery. I do delicate experiments here, and it wouldn't take much of a blow to spoil them. That's why those cords were cut."

"Who did it? Do you think Andy Foger——"

"No, I think it was the man Koku thought was a chicken thief, and whom we chased the other night. I've got to be on my guard. I wonder if——"

Tom was interrupted by the appearance of Koku, who came out of the shop with a letter the postman had just left.

"I don't know that writing very well, and yet it looks familiar," said Tom, as he tore open the missive. "Hello, here's more trouble!" he exclaimed as he hastily read it.

"What's up now?" asked Ned.

"This is from Mr. Period, the picture man," went on the young inventor. It's a warning."

"A warning?"

"Yes. He says:

" 'Dear Tom. Be on your guard. I understand that a rival moving picture concern is after you. They want to make you an offer, and get you away from me. But I trust you. Don't have anything to do with these other fellows. And, at the same time, don't give them a hint as to our plans. Don't tell them anything about your new camera. There is a lot of jealousy and rivalry in this business and they are all after me. They'll probably come to see you, but be on your guard. They know that I have been negotiating with you. Remember the alarm the other night.' "

CHAPTER VI

TRYING THE CAMERA

"WELL, what do you think of that?" cried Ned, as his chum finished.

"It certainly isn't very pleasant," replied Tom. "I wonder why those chaps can't let me alone? Why don't they invent cameras of their own? Why are they always trying to get my secret inventions?"

"I suppose they can't do things for themselves," answered Ned. " And then, again, your machinery always works, Tom, and some that your rivals make, doesn't."

"Well, maybe that's it," admitted our hero, as he put away the letter. "I will be on the watch, just as I have been before. I've got the burglar alarm wires adjusted on the shop now, and when these rival moving picture men come after me they'll get a short answer."

For several days nothing happened, and Tom and Ned worked hard on the Wizard Camera. It was nearing completion, and they were plan-

51

ning, soon, to give it a test, when, one afternoon,
two strangers, in a powerful automobile, came
to the Swift homestead. They inquired for Tom,
and, as he was out in the shop, with Ned and
Koku, and as he often received visitors out there,
Mrs. Baggert sent out the two men, who left
their car in front of the house.

As usual, Tom had the inner door to his shop
locked, and when Koku brought in a message
that two strangers would like to see the young inventor, Tom remarked:

"I guess it's the rival picture men, Ned. We'll
see what they have to say."

"Which of you is Tom Swift?" asked the
elder of the two men, as Tom and Ned entered
the front office, for our hero knew better than to
admit the strangers to the shop.

"I am," replied Tom.

"Well, we're men of business," went on the
speaker, "and there is no use beating about the
bush. I am Mr. Wilson Turbot, and this is my
partner, Mr. William Eckert. We are in the
business of making moving picture films, and I
understand that you are associated with Mr.
Period in this line. 'Spotty' we call him."

"Yes, I am doing some work for Mr. Period,"
admitted Tom, cautiously.

"Have you done any yet?"

"No, but I expect to."

"What kind of a camera are you going to use?" asked Mr. Eckert eagerly.

"I must decline to answer that," replied Tom, a bit stiffly.

"Oh, that's all right," spoke Mr. Turbot, good naturedly. "Only 'Spotty' was bragging that you were making a new kind of film for him, and we wondered if it was on the market."

"We are always looking for improvements," added Mr. Eckert.

"This camera isn't on the market," replied Tom, on his guard as to how he answered.

The two men whispered together for a moment, and then Mr. Turbot said:

"Well, as I remarked, we're men of business, and there's no use beating about the bush. We've heard of you, Tom Swift, and we know you can do things. Usually, in this world, every man has his price, and we're willing to pay big to get what we want. I don't know what offer Mr. Period made to you, but I'll say this: We'll give you double what he offered, for the exclusive rights to your camera, whenever it's on the market, and we'll pay you a handsome salary to work for us."

"I'm sorry, but I can't consider the offer," replied Tom firmly. "I have given my word to

Mr. Period. I have a contract with him, and I cannot break it."

"Offer him three times what Period did," said Mr. Eckert, in a hoarse whisper that Tom heard.

"It would be useless!" exclaimed our hero. "I wouldn't go back on my word for a hundred times the price I am to get. I am not in this business so much for the money, as I am for the pleasure of it."

The men were silent a moment. There were ugly looks on their faces. They looked sharply at Tom and Ned. Then Mr. Eckert said:

"You'll regret this, Tom Swift. We are the biggest firm of moving picture promoters in the world. We always get what we want."

"You won't get my camera," replied Tom calmly.

"I don't know about that!" exclaimed Mr. Turbot, as he made a hasty stride toward Tom, who stood in front of the door leading to the shop—the shop where his camera, almost ready for use, was on a bench. "I guess if we——"

"Koku!" suddenly called Tom.

The giant stepped into the front office. He had been standing near the door, inside the main shop. Mr. Turbot who had stretched forth his hand, as though to seize Tom, and his companion, who had advanced toward Ned, fairly jumped back in fright at the sight of the big man.

"Koku," went on Tom, in even tones, "just show these *gentlemen* to the front door—and *lock* it after them," he added significantly, as he turned back into the shop, followed by Ned.

"Yes, Mr. Tom," answered the giant, and then, with his big hand, and brawny fist, he gently turned the two men toward the outer door. They were gasping in surprise as they looked at the giant.

"You'll be sorry for this, Tom Swift!" exclaimed Mr. Turbot. "You'll regret not having taken our offer. This Period chat is only a small dealer. We can do better by you. You'll regret——"

"*You'll* regret coming here again," snapped Tom, as he closed the door of his shop, leaving Koku to escort the baffled plotters to their auto. Shortly afterward Tom and Ned heard the car puffing away.

"Well, they came, just as Mr. Period said they would," spoke Tom, slowly.

"Yes, and they went away again!" exclaimed Ned with a laugh. "They had their trip for nothing. Say, did you see how they stared at Koku?"

"Yes, he's a helper worth having, in cases like these."

Tom wrote a full account of what had happened and sent it to Mr. Period. He received in reply a few words, thanking him for his loyalty, and again warning him to be on his guard.

In the meanwhile, work went on rapidly on the Wizard Camera. Briefly described it was a small square box, with a lens projecting from it. Inside, however, was complicated machinery, much too complicated for me to describe. Tom Swift had put in his best work on this wonderful machine. As I have said, it could be worked by a storage battery, by ordinary electric current from a dynamo, or by hand. On top was a new kind of electric light. This was small and compact, but it threw out powerful beams. With the automatic arrangement set, and the light turned on, the camera could be left at a certain place after dark, and whatever went on in front of it would be reproduced on the moving roll of film inside.

In the morning the film could be taken out, developed, and the pictures thrown on a screen in the usual way, familiar to all who have been in a moving picture theatre. With the reproducing machines Tom had nothing to do, as they were already perfected. His task had been to make the new-style camera, and it was nearly completed.

'A number of rolls of films could be packed into the camera, and they could be taken out, or inserted, in daylight. Of course after one film had been made, showing any particular scene any number of films could be made from this "master" one. Just as is done with the ordinary moving picture camera. Tom had an attachment to show when one roll was used, and when another needed inserting.

For some time after the visit of the rival moving picture men, Tom was on his guard. Both house and shop were fitted with burglar alarms, but they did not ring. Eradicate and Koku were told to be on watch, but there was nothing for them to do.

"Well," remarked Tom to Ned, one afternoon, when they had both worked hard, "I think it's about finished. Of course it needs polishing, and there may be some adjusting to do, but my camera is now ready to take pictures—at least I'm going to give it a test."

"Have you the rolls of films?"

"Yes, half a dozen of 'em And I'm going to try the hardest test first."

"Which one is that?"

"The night test. I'm going to place the camera out in the yard, facing my shop. Then you and I, and some of the others, will go out, pass in front of it, do various stunts, and, in the morning we'll develop the films and see what we have."

"Why, are you going to leave the camera out all night?"

"Sure. I'm going to give it the hardest kind of a test."

"But are you and I going to stay up all night to do stunts in front of it?"

"No, indeed. I'm going to let it take whatever pictures happen to come along to be taken, after we get through making some special early ones. You see my camera will be a sort of watch dog, only of course it won't catch any one—that is, only their images will be caught on the film.

"Oh, I see," exclaimed Ned, and then he helped Tom fix the machine for the test.

CHAPTER VII

WHAT THE CAMERA CAUGHT

"WELL, is she working, Tom?" asked our hero's chum, a little later, when they had set the camera up on a box in the garden. It pointed toward the main shop door, and from the machine came a clicking sound. The electric light was glowing.

"Yes, it's all ready," replied Tom. "Now just act as if it wasn't there. You walk toward the shop. Do anything you please. Pretend you are coming in to see me on business. Act as if it was daytime. I'll stand here and receive you. Later, I'll get dad out here, Koku and Eradicate. I wish Mr. Period was here to see the test, but perhaps it's just as well for me to make sure it works before he sees it."

"All right, Tom, here I come."

Ned advanced toward the shop. He tried to act as though the camera was not taking pictures of him, at the rate of several a second, but he forgot himself, and turned to look at the staring lens. Then Tom, with a laugh, advanced to meet him, shaking hands with him. Then the lads indulged in a little skylarking. They threw snowballs at each other, taking care, however to keep within range of the lens. Of course when Tom worked the camera himself, he could point it wherever he wanted to, but it was now automatic.

Then the lads went to the shop, and came out again. They did several other things. Later Koku, and Eradicate did some "stunts," as Tom called them. Mr. Swift, too, was snapped, but Mrs. Baggert refused to come out.

"Well, I guess that will do for now," said Tom, as he stopped the mechanism. "I've just thought of something," he added. "If I leave the light burning, it will scare away, before they got in front of the lens, any one who might come along. I'll have to change that part of it."

"How can you fix it?" asked Ned.

"Easily. I'll rig up some flash lights, just ordinary photographing flashlights, you know. I'll time them to go off one after the other, and connect them with an electric wire to the door of my shop."

"Then your idea is——" began Ned.

"That some rascals may try to enter my shop at night. Not this particular night, but any night.

If they come to-night we'll be ready for them."

"An' can't yo'-all take a picture ob de chicken coop?" asked Eradicate. "Dat feller may come back t' rob mah hens."

"With the lens pointing toward the shop," spoke Tom, "it will also take snap shots of any one who tries to enter the coop. So, if the chicken thief *does* come, Rad, we'll have a picture of him."

Tom and Ned soon had the flashlights in place, and then they went to bed, listening, at times, for the puff that would indicate that the camera was working. But the night passed without incident, rather to Tom's disappointment. However, in the morning, he developed the film of the first pictures taken in the evening. Soon they were dry enough to be used in the moving picture machine, which Tom had bought, and set up in a dark room.

"There we are!" he cried, as the first images were thrown on the white screen. "As natural as life, Ned! My camera works all right!"

"That's so. Look! There's where I hit you with a snowball!" cried his chum, as the sky-larking scene was reached.

"Mah goodness!" cried Eradicate, when he saw himself walking about on the screen, as large as life. "Dat shorely am wonderful."

By the use of alcohol and an electric fan Tom soon had the films dry enough to use. Then the moving picture machine was set up in a dark room, and all gathered to see what would be thrown on the screen, greatly enlarged.

First came several brilliant flashes of light, and then, as the entrance to the shop loomed into view, a dark figure seemed to walk across the canvas. But it did not stop at the shop door. Instead it went to the chicken coop, and, as the man reached that door, he began working to get it open. Of course it had all taken place in a few seconds, for, as soon as the flashlights went off, the intruders had run away. But they had been there long enough to have their pictures taken.

The man at the chicken coop turned around as the lights flashed, and he was looking squarely at the camera. Of course this made his face very plain to the audience, as Tom turned the crank of the reproducing machine.

"Why, it's a colored man!" cried Ned in surprise.

"Yes, I guess it's only an ordinary chicken thief, after all," remarked Tom.

There was a gasp from Eradicate.

"Fo' de land sakes!" he cried. "De raskil! Ef dat ain't mah own second cousin, what libs

down by de ribber! An' to t'ink dat Samuel
'Rastus Washington Jackson Johnson, mah own
second cousin, should try t' rob *mah* chicken
coop! Oh, won't I gib it t' him!"

"Are you sure, Rad?" asked Tom.

"Suah? Sartin I'se suah, Massa Tom," was
the answer as the startled colored man on the
screen stared at the small audience. "I'd know
dat face ob his'n anywhere."

"Well, I guess he's the only one we caught last
night," said Tom, as the disappointed chicken
thief ran away, and so out of focus. But the
next instant there came another series of flash-
light explosions on the screen, and there, almost
as plainly as if our friends were looking at them,
they saw two men stealthily approaching the
shop. They, too, as the chicken thief had done,
tried the door, and then, they also, startled by the
flashes, turned around.

"Look!" cried Ned.

"Great Scott!" exclaimed Tom. "Those are
the two rivals of Mr. Period! They are Mr. Turbot and Mr. Eckert!"

"Same men I pushed out!" cried Koku, much
excited.

There was no doubt of it, and, as the images
faded from the screen, caused by the men running away, Tom and Ned realized that their

rivals had tried to put their threat into execution—the threat of making Tom wish he had taken their offer.

"I guess they came to take my camera,—but, nstead the camera took them," said the young inventor grimly.

CHAPTER VIII

PHOTOS FROM THE AIRSHIP

"WELL, Tom, how is it going?" asked a voice in the door of the shop where the young inventor was working. He looked up quickly to behold Mr. Nestor, father of Mary, in which young lady, as I have said, Tom was much interested. "How is the moving picture camera coming on?"

"Pretty good, Mr. Nestor. Come in. I guess Koku knew you all right. I told him to let in any of my friends, but I have to keep him there on guard."

"So I understand. They nearly got in the other night, but I hear that your camera caught *them*."

"Yes, that proved that the machine is a success, even if we didn't succeed in arresting the men."

"Did you try?"

"Yes, I sent copies of the film, showing Turbot and Eckert trying to break into my shop, to Mr.

Period, and he had enlarged photographs made, and went to the police. They said it was rather flimsy evidence on which to arrest anybody, and so they didn't act. However, we sent copies of the pictures to Turbot and Eckert themselves, so *they* know that *we* know they were here, and I guess they'll steer clear of me after this."

"I guess so, Tom," agreed Mr. Nestor with a laugh. "But what about the chicken thief?"

"Oh, Eradicate attended to his second cousin. He went to see him, showed him a print from the film, and gave him to understand that he'd be blown up with dynamite, or kicked by Boomerang, if he ever came around here again, and so Samuel 'Rastus Washington Jackson Johnson will be careful about visiting strange chicken coops, after this."

"I believe you, Tom. But how is the camera coming on?"

"Very well. I am making a few changes in it, and I expect to get my biggest airship in readiness for the trip in about a week, and then I'll try taking pictures from her. But I understand that you are interested in Mr. Period's business, Mr. Nestor?"

"Yes, I own some stock in the company, and, Tom, that's what I came over to see you about. I need a vacation. Mary and her mother are going away this Spring for a long visit, and I was wondering if you couldn't take me with you on the trips you will make to get moving pictures for our concern."

"Of course I can, Mr. Nestor. "I'll be glad to do it."

"And there is another thing, Tom," went on Mr. Nestor, soberly. "I've got a good deal of my fortune tied up in this moving picture affair. I want to see you win out—I don't want our rivals to get ahead of us."

"They shan't get ahead of us."

"You see, Tom, it's this way. There is a bitter fight on between our concern and that controlled by our rivals. Each is trying to get the business of a large chain of moving picture theatres throughout the United States. These theatre men are watching us both, and the contracts for next season will go to the concern showing the best line of films. If our rivals get ahead of us— well, it will just about ruin our company,—and about ruin me too, I guess."

"I shall do my very best," answered our hero.

"Is Mr. Damon going along?"

"Well, I have just written to ask him. I sent the letter yesterday.

"Doesn't he know what you contemplate?"

"Not exactly. You see when he came, that

time I was overcome by the fumes from the acids, everything was so upset that I didn't get a chance to tell him. He's been away on business ever since, but returned yesterday. I certainly hope that he goes with us. Ned Newton is coming, and with you, and Koku and myself, it will be a nice party."

"Then you are going to take Koku?"

"I think I will. I'm a little worried about what these rival moving picture men might do, and if I get into trouble with them, my giant helper would come in very useful, to pick one up and throw him over a tree top, for instance."

"Indeed, yes," agreed Mr. Nestor, with a laugh. "But I hope nothing like that happens."

"Nothing like that happens?" suddenly asked a voice. "Bless my bookcase! but there always seems to be *something* going on here. What's up now, Tom Swift?"

"Nothing much, Mr. Damon," replied our hero, as he recognized his odd friend. "We were just talking about moving pictures, Mr. Damon, and about you. Did you get my letter?"

"I did, Tom."

"And are you going wth us?"

"Tom, did you ever know me to refuse an invitation from you? I guess not! Of *course* I'm going. But, for mercy sakes, don't tell my wife!

She mustn't know about it until the last minute, and then she'll be so surprised, when I tell her, that she won't think of objecting. Don't let her know."

Tom laughed, and promised, and then the three began talking of the prospective trip. After a bit Ned Newton joined the party.

Tom showed the two men how his new camera worked. He had made several improvements on it since the first pictures were taken, and now it was almost perfect. Mr. Period had been out to see it work, and said it was just the apparatus needed.

"You can get films with that machine," he said, "that will be better than any pictures ever thrown on a screen. My fortune will be made, Tom, and yours too, if you can only get pictures that are out of the ordinary. There will be some hair-raising work, I expect, but you can do it."

"I'll try," spoke Tom. "I have——"

"Hold on! I know what you are going to say," interrupted Mr. Period. "You are going to say that you've gone through some strenuous times already. I know you have, but you're going to have more soon. I think I'll send you to India first."

"To India!" exclaimed Tom, for Mr. Period

had spoken of that as if it was but a journey downtown.

"Yes, India. I want a picture of an elephant drive, and if you can get pictures of the big beasts in a stampede, so much the better. Then, too, the Durbar is on now, and that will make a good film. How soon can you start for Calcutta?"

"Well, I've got to overhaul the airship," said Tom. "That will take about three weeks. The camera is practically finished. I can leave in a month, I guess."

"Good. We'll have fine weather by that time Are you going all the way by your airship?"

"No, I think it will be best to take that apart ship it by steamer, and go that way ourselves. I can put the airship together in India, and then use it to get to any other part of Europe, Asia or Africa you happen to want pictures from."

"Good! Well, get to work now, and I'll see you again."

In the days that followed, Tom and Ned were kept busy. There was considerable to do on the airship, in the way of overhauling it. This craft was Tom's largest, and was almost like the one in which he had gone to the caves of ice, where it was wrecked. It had been, however, much improved.

The craft was a sort of combined dirigible

balloon, and aeroplane, and could be used as either. There was a machine on board for generating gas, to use in the balloon part of it, and the ship, which was named the *Flyer,* could carry several persons.

"Bless my shoe laces!" cried Mr. Damon one day as he looked at Koku. "If we take him along in the airship, will we be able to float, Tom?"

"Oh, yes. The airship is plenty big enough. Besides, we are not going to take along a very large party, and the camera is not heavy. Oh, we'll be all right. I suppose you'll be on hand to-morrow, Mr. Damon?"

"To-morrow? What for?"

"We're going to take the picture machine up in the airship, and get some photos from the sky. I expect to make some films from high in the air, as well as some in the regular way, on the ground, and I want a little practice. Come around about two o'clock, and we'll have a trial flight."

"All right. I will. But don't let my wife know I'm going up in an airship again. She's read of so many accidents lately, that she's nervous about having me take a trip."

"Oh, I won't tell," promised Tom with a laugh, and he worked away harder than ever, for there were many little details to perfect. The weather was now getting warm, as there was an early spring, and it was pleasant out of doors.

The moving picture camera was gotten in readiness. Extra rolls of films were on hand, and the big airship, in which they were to go up, for their first test of taking pictures from high in the air, had been wheeled out of the shed.

"Are you going up very far?" asked Mr. Nestor of Tom, and the young inventor thought that Mary's father was a trifle nervous. He had not made many flights, and then only a little way above the ground, with Tom.

"Not very high," replied our hero. "You see I want to get pictures that will be large, and if I'm too far away I can't do it."

"Glad to hear it, replied Mr. Nestor, with a note of relief in his voice. "Though I suppose to fall a thousand feet isn't much different from falling a hundred when you consider the results."

"Not much," admitted Tom frankly.

"Bless my feather bed!" cried Mr. Damon. "Please don't talk of falling, when we're going up in an airship. It makes me nervous."

"We'll not fall!" declared Tom confidently.

Mr. Period sent his regrets, that he could not be present at the trial, stating in his letter that he was the busiest man in the world, and that his time was worth about a dollar a minute just at present. He, however, wished Tom all success.

Tom's first effort was to sail along, with the lens of the camera pointed straight toward the earth. He would thus get, if successful, a picture that, when thrown on the screen, would give the spectators the idea that they were looking down from a moving balloon. For that reason Tom was not going to fly very high, as he wanted to get all the details possible.

"All aboard!" cried the young inventor, when he had seen to it that his airship was in readiness for a flight. The camera had been put aboard, and the lens pointed toward earth through a hole in the main cabin floor. All who were expected to make the trip with Tom were on hand, Koku taking the place of Eradicate this time, as the colored man was too aged and feeble to go along.

"All ready?" asked Ned, who stood in the steering tower, with his hand on the starting lever, while Tom was at the camera to see that it worked properly.

"All ready," answered the young inventor, and, an instant later, they shot upward, as the big propellers whizzed around.

Tom at once started the camera to taking pictures rapidly, as he wanted the future audience to get a perfect idea of how it looked to go up in a balloon, leaving the earth behind. Then as the *Flyer* moved swiftly over woods and fields, Tom moved the lens from side to side, to get different views.

"Say! This is great!" cried Mr. Nestor, to whom air-riding was much of a novelty. "Are you getting good pictures, Tom?"

"I can't tell until we develope them. But the machine seems to be working all right. I'm going to sail back now, and get some views of our own house from up above."

They had sailed around the town of Shopton, to the neighboring villages, over woods and fields. Now they were approaching Shopton again.

"Bless my heart!" suddenly exclaimed Mr. Damon, who was looking toward the earth, as they neared Tom's house.

"What is it?" asked our hero, glancing up from the picture machine, the registering dial of which he was examining.

"Look there! At your shop, Tom! There seems to be a lot of smoke coming from it!"

They were almost over Tom's shop now, and, as Mr. Damon had said, there was considerable smoke rolling above it.

"I guess Eradicate is burning up papers and trash," was Ned's opinion.

Tom looked to where the camera pointed. He

was right over his shop now, and could see a dense vapor issuing from the door.

"That isn't Eradicate!" cried the young inventor. "My shop is on fire! I've got to make a quick drop, and save it! There are a lot of valuable models, and machines in there! Send us down, Ned, as fast as she'll go!"

CHAPTER IX

OFF FOR INDIA

"Bless my hose reel!" cried Mr. Damon, as the airship took a quick lurch toward the earth. "Things are always hapening to you, Tom Swift! Your shop on fire! How did it happen?"

"Look!" suddenly cried Ned, before Tom had a chance to answer. "There's a man running away from the shop, Tom!"

All saw him, and, as the airship rushed downward it could be seen that he was a fellow dressed in ragged garments, a veritable tramp.

"I guess that fire didn't *happen*," said Tom significantly. "It was deliberately set. Oh, if we can only get there before it gains too much headway!"

"I like to catch that fellow!" exclaimed Koku, shaking his big fist at the retreating tramp. "I fix him!"

On rushed the airship, and the man who had probably started the fire, glanced up at it. Tom suddenly turned the lens of his Wizard Camera toward him. The mechanism inside, which had

78

been stopped, started clicking again, as the young inventor switched on the electric current.

"What are you doing?" cried Ned, as he guided the airship toward the shop, whence clouds of smoke were rolling.

"Taking his picture," replied Tom. "It may come in useful for evidence."

But he was not able to get many views of the fellow, for the latter must have suspected what was going on. He quickly made a dive for the bushes, and was soon lost to sight. Tom shut off his camera.

"Bless my life preserver!" cried Mr. Damon. "There comes your father, Tom, and Mrs. Baggert! They've got buckets! They're going to put out the fire!"

"Why don't they think to use the hose?" cried the young inventor, for he had his shop equipped with many hose lines, and an electrically driven pump. The hose! The hose, dad!" shouted Tom, but it is doubtful if his father or Mrs. Baggert heard him, for the engine of the airship was making much noise. However, the two with the buckets looked up, and waved their hands to those on the *Flyer*.

"There's Eradicate!" yelled Ned. "He's got the hose all right!" The colored man was beginning to unreel a line.

"That's what it needs!" exclaimed Tom. "Now there's some chance to save the shop."

"We'll be there ourselves to take a hand in a few seconds!" cried Mr. Damon, forgetting to bless anything.

"The scoundrel who started this fire, and those back of him, ought to be imprisoned for life!" declared Mr. Nestor.

A moment later Ned had landed the airship within a short distance of the shop. In an instant the occupants of the craft had leaped out, and Tom, after a hasty glance to see that his valuable camera was safe, dashed toward the building crying:

"Never mind the pails, dad! Use the hose! There's a nozzle at the back door. Go around there, and play the water on from that end."

Eradicate, with his line of hose, had disappeared into the shop through the front door, and the others pressed in after him, heedless of the dense smoke.

"Is it blazing much, Rad?" cried Tom.

"Can't see no blaze at all, Massa Tom," replied the colored man. "Dere's a heap of suffin in de middle ob de flo', an' dat's what's raisin' all de rumpus."

They all saw it a moment later, a smouldering heap of rags and paper on the concrete floor of

the shop. Eradicate turned his hose on it, there
was a hissing sound, a cloud of steam arose, and
the fire was practically out, though much smoke
remained.

"Jove! that was a lucky escape!" exclaimed
Tom, as he looked around when the vapor had
partly cleared away. "No damage done at all,
as far as I can see. I wonder what the game
was? Did you see anything of a tramp around
here?" he asked of his father.

"No, Tom. I have been busy in the house.
So has Mrs. Baggert. Suddenly she called my
attention to the smoke coming from the door,
and we ran out."

"I seen it, too," added Eradicate. "I was doin'
some whitewashin', an' I run up as soon as I
could."

"We saw the tramp all right, but he got
away," said Tom, and he told how he had taken
pictures of him. "I don't believe it would be
much use to look for him now, though."

"Me look," spoke Koku significantly, as he
hurried off in the direction taken by the tramp.
He came back later, not having found him.

"What do you think of it, Tom?" asked Ned,
when the excitement had calmed down, and the
pile of burned rags had been removed. It was

found that oil and chemicals had been put on them to cause a dense smoke.

"I think it was the work of those fellows who are after my camera," replied the young inventor. "They are evidently watching me, and when they saw us all go off in the airship they thought probably that the coast was clear."

"But why should they start a fire?"

"I don't know, but probably to create a lot of smoke, and excitement, so that they could search, and not be detected. Maybe the fellow after he found that the camera was gone, wanted to draw those in the house out to the shop, so he could have a clear field to search in my room for any drawings that would give him a clew as to how my machine works. They certainly did not want to burn the shop, for that pile of rags could have smouldered all day on the concrete floor, without doing any harm. Robbery was the motive, I think."

"The police ought to be notified," declared Mr. Nestor. "Develope those pictures, Tom, and I'll take the matter up with the police. Maybe they can identify the tramp from the photographs."

But this proved impossible. Tom had secured several good films, not only in the first views he took, giving the spectators the impression that they were going up in an airship, but also those showing the shop on fire, and the tramp running away, were very plain.

The police made a search for the incendiary, but of course did not find him. Mr. Period came to Shopton, and declared it was his belief that his rivals, Turbot and Eckert, had had a hand in the matter. But it was only a suspicion, though Tom himself believed the same thing. Still nothing could be accomplished.

"The thing to do, now that the camera works all right, is for you to hit the trail for India at once," suggested the picture man. "They won't follow you there. Get me some pictures of the Durbar, of elephants being captured, of tiger fights, anything exciting."

"I'll do my——" began Tom.

"Wait, I'm not through," interrupted the excitable man. "Then go get some volcanoes, earthquakes—anything that you think would be interesting. I'll keep in touch with you, and cable occasionally. Get all the films you can. When will you start?"

"I can leave inside of two weeks," replied Tom.

"Then do it, and, meanwhile, be on your guard."

It was found that a few changes were needed

on the camera. And some adjustments to the airship. Another trial flight was made, and some excellent pictures taken. Then Tom and his friends prepared to take the airship apart, and pack it for shipment to Calcutta. It was to go on the same steamer as themselves, and of course the Wizard Camera would accompany Tom. He took along many rolls of films, enough, he thought, for many views. He was also to send back to Mr. Period from time to time, the exposed rolls of film, so they could be developed, and printed in the United States, as Tom would not have very good facilities for this on the airship, and to reproduce them there was almost out of the question. Still he did fit up a small dark room aboard the *Flyer,* where he could develope pictures if he wished.

There was much to be done, but hard work accomplished it, and finally the party was ready to start for India. Tom said good-bye to Mary Nestor, of course, and her father accompanied our hero from the Nestor house to the Swift homestead, where the start was to take place.

Eradicate bade his master a tearful good-bye, and there was moisture in the eyes of Mr. Swift, as he shook hands with his son.

"Take care of yourself, Tom," he said. "Don't run too many risks. This moving picture taking isn't as easy as it sounds. It's more than just pointing your camera at things. Write if you get a chance, or send me a message."

Tom promised, and then bade farewell to Mrs. Baggert. All were assembled, Koku, Mr. Damon, who blessed everything he saw, and some things he did not, Ned, Mr. Nestor and Tom. The five were to go by train to New York, there to go aboard the steamer.

Their journey to the metropolis was uneventful. Mr. Period met them at the steamship dock, after Tom had seen to it that the baggage, and the parts of the airship were safely aboard.

"I wish I were going along!" exclaimed the picture man. "It's going to be a great trip. But I can't spare the time. I'm the busiest man in the world. I lose about a thousand dollars just coming down to see you off, but it's a good investment. I don't mind it. Now, Tom, good luck, and don't forget, I want exciting views."

"I'll try——" began our hero.

"Wait, I know what you're going to say!" interrupted Mr. Period. "You'll do it, of course. Well, I must be going. I will—Great Scott!" and Mr. Period interrupted himself. "He has the nerve to come here!"

"Who?" asked Tom.

"Wilson Turbot, the rascal! He's trying to

balk me at the last minute, I believe. I'm going to see what he means!" and with this, the excited Mr. Period rushed down the gangplank, toward the man at whom he had pointed—one of the men who had tried to buy Tom's picture taking camera.

A moment later the steamer's whistle blew, the last belated passenger rushed up the gangplank, it was drawn in, and the vessel began to move away from the dock. Tom and his friends were on their way to India, and the last glimpse they had of Mr. Period was as he was chasing along the pier, after Mr. Turbot.

CHAPTER X

UNEXPECTED EXCITEMENT

"WELL, what do you know about that, Tom?" asked Ned, as they stood on deck watching the chase. "Isn't he the greatest ever—Mr. Period, I mean?"

"He certainly is. I'd like to see what happens when he catches that Turbot chap."

"Bless my pocket handkerchief!" cried Mr. Damon. "I don't believe he will. Mr. Period's legs aren't long enough for fast running."

"Those scoundrels were after us, up to the last minute," spoke Mr. Nestor, as the ship moved farther out from the dock. Tom and his friends could no longer see the excitable picture man after his rival, but there was a commotion in the crowd, and it seemed as if he had caught the fellow.

"Well, we're free of him now," spoke the young inventor, with a breath of relief. "That is, unless they have set some one else on our trail," and he looked carefully at the passengers near him, to detect, if possible, any who might look like spies in the pay of the rival moving picture concern, or any suspicious characters who might try to steal the valuable camera, that was now safely locked in Tom's cabin. Our hero, however, saw no one to worry about. He resolved to remain on his guard.

Friends and relatives were waving farewells to one another, and the band was playing, as the big vessel drew out into the North, or Hudson, river, and steamed for the open sea.

Little of interest marked the first week of the voyage. All save Koku had done much traveling before, and it was no novelty to them. The giant, however, was amused and delighted with everything, even the most commonplace things he saw. He was a source of wonder to all the other passengers, and, in a way, he furnished much excitement.

One day several of the sailors were on deck, shifting one of the heavy anchors. They went about it in their usual way, all taking hold, and "heaving" together with a "chanty," or song, to enliven their work. But they did not make much progress, and one of the mates got rather excited about it.

"Here, shiver my timbers!" he cried. "Lively now! Lay about you, and get that over to the side!"

"Yo! Heave! Ho!" called the leader of the sailor gang.

The anchor did not move, for it had either caught on some projection, or the men were not using their strength.

"Lively! Lively!" cried the mate.

Suddenly Koku, who was in the crowd of passengers watching the work, pushed his way to where the anchor lay. With a powerful, but not rough action, he shoved the sailors aside. Then, stooping over, he took a firm grip of the big piece of iron, planted his feet well apart on the deck, and lifted the immense mass in his arms. There was a round of applause from the group of passengers.

"Where you want him?" Koku calmly asked of the mate, as he stood holding the anchor.

"Blast my marlin spikes!" cried the mate. "I never see the like of this afore! Put her over there, shipmate. If I had you on a voyage or two *you'd* be running the ship, instead of letting the screw push her along. Put her over there," and he indicated where he wanted the anchor.

Koku calmly walked along the deck, laid the anchor down as if it was an ordinary weight, and passed over to where Tom stood looking on in amused silence. Ther were murmurs of surprise from the passengers at the giant's strength, and the sailors went forward much abashed.

"Say, I'd give a good bit to have a bodyguard like that," exclaimed a well-known millionaire passenger, who, it was reported, was in constant fear of attacks, though they had never taken place. "I wonder if I could get him."

He spoke to Tom about it, but our hero would not listen to a proposition to part with Koku. Besides, it is doubtful if the simple giant would leave the lad who had brought him away from his South American home. But, if Koku was wonderfully strong, and, seemingly afraid of nothing, there were certain things he feared.

One afternoon, for the amusement of the passengers, a net was put overboard, sunk to a considerable depth, and hauled up with a number of fishes in it. Some of the finny specimens were good for eating, and others were freaks, strange and curious.

Koku was in the throng that gathered on deck to look at the haul. Suddenly a small fish, but very hideous to look at, leaped from the net and flopped toward the giant. With a scream of fear Koku jumped to one side, and ran down to his stateroom. He could not be induced to come on deck until Tom assured him that the fishes had been disposed of. Thus Koku was a mixture of giant and baby. But he was a general favorite on the ship, and often gave exhibitions of his strength.

Meanwhile Tom and his friends had been on the lookout for any one who might be trailing them. But they saw no suspicious characters among the passengers, and, gradually, they began to feel that they had left their enemies behind.

The weather was pleasant, and the voyage very enjoyable. Tom and the others had little to do, and they were getting rather impatient for the time to come when they could put the airship together, and sail off over the jungle, to get moving pictures of the elephants.

"Have you any films in the camera now?" asked Ned of his chum on day, as they sat on deck together.

"Yes, it's all ready for instant use. Even the storage battery is charged. Why?"

"Oh, I was just wondering. I was thinking we might somehow see something we could take pictures of."

"Not much out here," said Tom, as he looked across the watery expanse. As he did so, he saw a haze of smoke dead ahead. "We'll pass a steamer soon," he went on, "but that wouldn't make a good picture. It's too common."

As the two lads watched, the smoke became blacker, and the cloud it formed grew much larger.

"They're burning a lot of coal on that ship," remarked Ned. "Must be trying for a speed record."

A little later a sailor stationed himself in the crow's nest, and focused a telescope on the smoke. An officer, on deck, seemed to be waiting for a report from the man aloft.

"That's rather odd," remarked Ned. "I never knew them to take so much interest in a passing steamer before; and we've gone by several of late."

"That's right," agreed Tom. "I wonder——"

At that moment the officer, looking up, called out:

"Main top!"

"Aye, aye, sir," answered the sailor with the glass. "She's a small steamer, sir, and she's on fire!"

"That's what I feared. Come down. I'll tell the captain. We must crowd on all steam, and go to the rescue."

"Did you hear that?" cried Ned to Tom, as the officer hurried to the bridge, where the captain awaited him. "A steamer on fire at sea, Tom! why don't you——"

I'm going to!" interrupted the young inventor, as he started for his cabin on the run. "I'm going to get some moving pictures of the rescue! That will be a film worth having."

A moment later the *Belchar,* the vessel on which our friends had embarked, increased her speed, while sudden excitement developed on board.

As the *Belchar* approached the burning steamer, which had evidently seen her, and was making all speed toward her, the cloud of smoke became more dense, and a dull flame could be seen reflected in the water.

"She's going fast!" cried Mr. Nestor, as he joined Ned on deck.

"Bless my insurance policy!" cried Mr. Damon. "What a strange happening! Where's Tom Swift?"

"Gone for his camera," answered his chum. "He's going to get some pictures of the rescue."

"All hands man the life boats!" cried an officer, and several sailors sprang to the davits, ready to lower the boats, when the steamers should be near enough together.

Up on deck came Tom, with his wonderful camera.

"Here you go, Ned!" he called. "Give me a hand. I'm going to start the film now."

CHAPTER XI

AN ELEPHANT STAMPEDE

"Lower away!"

"Stand by the life boats!"

"Let go! Pull hearty!"

These and other commands marked the beginning of the rescue, as the sailors manned the davit-falls, and put the boats into the water. The burning steamer had now come to a stop, not far away from the *Belchar*, which was also lay-to. There was scarcely any sea running, and no wind, so that the work of rescuing was not difficult from an ordinary standpoint. But there was grave danger, because the fire on the doomed vessel was gaining rapidly.

"That's oil burning," remarked an officer, and it seemed so, from the dense clouds of smoke that rolled upward.

"Is she working, Tom?" asked Ned, as he helped his chum to hold the wonderful camera steady on the rail, so that a good view of the burning steamer could be had.

94

"Yes, the film is running. Say, I wonder if they'll get 'em all off?"

"Oh, I think so. There aren't many passengers. I guess it's a tramp freighter."

They could look across the gap of water, and see the terrified passengers and crew crowding to the rail, holding out their hands appealingly to the brave sailors who were lustily and rapidly pulling toward them in life boats.

At times a swirl of smoke would hide those on the doomed vessel from the sight of the passengers on the *Belchar,* and on such occasions the frightened screams of women could be heard. Once, as the smoke cleared away, a woman, with a child in her arms, giving a backward glance toward the flames that were now enveloping the stern of the vessel, attempted to leap overboard.

Many hands caught her, however, and all this was registered on the film of Tom's camera, which was working automatically. As the two vessels drifted along, Tom and Ned shifted the lens so as to keep the burning steamer, and the approaching lifeboats, in focus.

"There's the first rescue!" cried Ned, as the woman who had attempted to leap overboard, was, with her child, carefully lowered into a boat. "Did you get that, Tom?"

"I certainly did. This will make a good picture. I think I'll send it back to Mr. Period as soon as we reach port."

"Maybe you could develop it on board here, and show it. I understand there's a dark room, and the captain said one of his officers, who used to be in the moving picture business, had a reproducing machine."

"Then that's what I'll do!" cried Tom. "I'll have our captain charge all the *Belchar* passengers admission, and we'll get up a fund for the fire sufferers. They'll probably lose all their baggage."

"That will be great!" exclaimed Ned.

The rescue was now in full swing, and, in a short time all the passengers and crew had been transferred to the life boats. Tom got a good picture of the captain of the burning steamer being the last to leave his vessel. Then the approaching life boats, with their loads of sailors, and rescued ones, were caught on the films.

"Are you all off?" cried the captain of the *Belchar* to the unfortunate skipper of the doomed ship.

"All off, yes, thank you. It is a mercy you were at hand. I have a cargo of oil. You had better stand off, for she'll explode in a few minutes."

"I must get a picture of that!" declared Tom,

as the *Belchar* got under way again. "That will cap the climax, and make a film that will be hard to beat."

A few moments later there was a tremendous explosion on the tramp oiler. A column of wreckage and black smoke shot skyward, and Tom secured a fine view of it. Then the wreck disappeared beneath the waves, while the rescuing steamer sailed on, with those who had been saved. They had brought off only the things they wore, for the fire had occurred suddenly, and spread rapidly. Kind persons aboard the *Belchar* looked after the unfortunates. Luckily there was not a large passenger list on the tramp. And the crew was comparatively small, so it was not hard work to make room for them, or take care of them, aboard the *Belchar*.

Tom developed his pictures, and produced them in one of the large saloons, on a machine he borrowed from the man of whom Ned had spoken. A dollar admission was charged, and the crowd was so large that Tom had to give two performances. The films, showing the burning steamer and the rescue, were excellent, and enough money was realized to aid, most substantially, the unfortunate passengers and crew.

A few days later a New York bound steamer was spoken, and on it Tom sent the roll of developed films to Mr. Period, with a letter of explanation.

I will not give all the details of the rest of the voyage. Sufficient to say that no accidents marred it, nor did Tom discover any suspicious characters aboard. In due time our friends arrived at Calcutta, and were met by an agent of Mr. Period, for he had men in all quarters of the world, making films for him.

This agent took Tom and his party to a hotel, and arranged to have the airship parts sent to a large open shed, not far away, where it could be put together. The wonderful scenes in the Indian city interested Tom and his companions for a time, but they had observed so many strange sights from time to time that they did not marvel greatly. Koku, however, was much delighted. He was like a child.

"What are you going to do first?" asked Ned, when they had recovered from the fatigue of the ocean voyage and had settled themselves in the hotel.

"Put the airship together," replied our hero, "and then, after getting some Durbar pictures, we'll head for the jungle. I want to get some elephant pictures, showing the big beasts being captured."

Mr. Period's agent was a great help to them

in this. He secured native helpers, who aided Tom in assembling the airship, and in a week or two it was ready for a flight. The wonderful camera, too, was looked over, and the picture agent said he had never seen a better one.

"It can take the kind of pictures I never could," he said. "I get Calcutta street scenes for Mr. Period, and occasionally I strike a good one. But I wish I had your chance."

Tom invited him to come along in the airship, but the agent, who only looked after Mr. Period's interests as a side issue, could not leave his work.

The airship was ready for a flight, stores and provisions had been put on board, there was enough gasoline for the motor, and gas for the balloon bag, to carry the *Flyer* thousands of miles. The moving picture camera had been tested after the sea voyage, and had been found to work perfectly. Many rolls of films were taken along. Tom got some fine views of the Durbar of India, and his airship created a great sensation.

"Now I guess we're all ready for the elephants," said Tom one day as he came back from an inspection of the airship as it rested in the big shed. "We'll start to-morrow morning, and head for the jungle."

Amid the cries from a throng of wondering and awed natives, and with the farewells of Mr.

Period's agent ringing in their ears, Tom and his party made an early start. The *Flyer* rose like a bird, and shot across the city, while on the house tops many people watches the strange sight. Tom did not start his camera working, as Mr. Period's agent said he had made many pictures of the Indian city, and even one taken from an airship, would not be much of a novelty.

Tom had made inquiries, and learned that by a day's travel in his airship (though it would have been much longer ordinarily) he could reach a jungle where elephants might be found. Of course there was nothing certain about it, as the big animals roamed all over, being in one district one day, and on the next, many miles off.

Gradually the city was left behind, and some time later the airship was sailing along over the jungle. After the start, when Ned and Tom, with Mr. Damon helping occasionally, had gotten the machinery into proper adjustment, the *Flyer* almost ran herself. Then Tom took his station forward, with his camera in readiness, and a powerful spyglass at hand, so that he might see the elephants from a distance.

He had been told that, somewhere in the district for which he was headed, an elephant drive was contemplated. He hoped to be on hand to get pictures of it, and so sent his airship ahead at top speed.

On and on they rode, being as much at ease in the air as they would have been if traveling in a parlor car. They did not fly high, as it was necessary to be fairly close to the earth to get good pictures.

"Well, I guess we won't have any luck to-day," remarked Ned, as night approached, and they had had no sight of the elephants. They had gone over mile after mile of jungle, but had seen few wild beasts in sufficient numbers to make it worth while to focus the camera on them.

"We'll float along to-night," decided Tom, "and try again in the morning."

It was about ten o'clock the next day, when Ned, who had relieved Tom on watch, uttered a cry:

"What is it?" asked his chum, as he rushed forward. "Has anything happened?"

"Lots!" cried Ned. "Look!" He pointed down below. Tom saw, crashing through the jungle, a big herd of elephants. Behind them, almost surrounding them, in fact, was a crowd of natives in charge of white hunters, who were driving the herd toward a stockade.

"There's a chance for a grand picture!" exclaimed Tom, as he got the camera ready. "Take charge of the ship, Ned. Keep her right over the big animals, and I'll work the camera."

Quickly he focused the lens on the strange scene below him. There was a riot of trumpeting from the elephants. The beaters and hunters shouted and yelled. Then they saw the airship and waved their hands to Tom and his friends, but whether to welcome them, or warn them away, could not be told.

The elephants were slowly advancing toward the stockade. Tom was taking picture after picture of them, when suddenly as the airship came lower, in response to a signal to Ned from the young inventor, one of the huge pachyderms looked up, and saw the strange sight. He might have taken it for an immense bird. At any rate he gave a trumpet of alarm, and the next minute, with screams of rage and fear, the elephants turned, and charged in a wild stampede on those who were driving them toward the stockade.

"Look!" cried Ned. "Those hunters and natives will be killed!"

"I'm afraid so!" shouted Tom, as he continued to focus his camera on the wonderful sight.

CHAPTER XII

THE LION FIGHT

CRASHING through the jungle the huge beasts turned against those who had been driving them on toward the stockade. With wild shouts and yells, the hunters and their native helpers tried to turn back the elephant tide, but it was useless. The animals had been frightened by the airship, and were following their leader, a big bull, that went crashing against great trees, snapping them off as if they were pipe stems.

"Say, this is something like!" cried Ned, as he guided the airship over the closely packed body of elephants, so Tom could get good pictures, for the herd had divided, and a small number had gone off with one of the other bulls.

"Yes, I'll get some great pictures," agreed Tom, as he looked in through a red covered opening in the camera, to see how much film was left.

The airship was now so low down that Tom, and the others, could easily make out the faces of the hunters, and the native helpers. One of the hunters, evidently the chief, shaking his fist at our hero, cried:

"Can't you take your blooming ship out of the way, my man? It's scaring the beasts, and we've been a couple of weeks on this drive. We don't want to lose all our work. Take your bloody ship away!"

"I guess he must be an Englishman," remarked Mr. Nestor, with a laugh.

"Bless my dictionary, I should say so," agreed Mr. Damon. "Bloody, blooming ship! The idea!"

"Well, I suppose we *have* scared the beasts," said Tom. "We ought to get out of the way. Put her up, Ned, and we'll come down some distance in advance."

"Why, aren't you going to take any more views of the elephants?"

"Yes, but I've got enough of a view from above. Besides, I've got to put in a fresh reel of film, and I might as well get out of their sight to do it. Maybe that will quiet them, and the hunters can turn them back toward the stockade. If they do, I have another plan."

"What is it?" his chum wanted to know.

"I'm going to make a landing, set up my camera at the entrance to the stockade, and get

a series of pictures as the animals come in. I
think that will be a novelty."

"That certainly will," agreed Mr. Nestor. "I
am sure Mr. Period will appreciate that. But
won't it be dangerous, Tom?"

"I suppose so, but I'm getting used to danger,"
replied our hero, with a laugh.

Ned put the ship high into the air, as Tom shut
off the power from the camera. Then the *Flyer*
was sent well on in advance of the stampede of
elephants, so they could no longer see it, or hear
the throb of the powerful engines. Tom hoped
that this would serve to quiet the immense
creatures.

As the travelers flew on, over the jungle, they
could still hear the racket made by the hunters
and beaters, and the shrill trumpeting of the elephants, as they crashed through the forest.

Tom at once began changing the film in the
camera, and Ned altered the course of the airship, to send it back toward the stockade, which
they had passed just before coming upon the
herd of elephants.

I presume most of my readers know what an
elephant drive is like. A stockade, consisting of
heavy trees, is made in the jungle. It is like the
old fashioned forts our forefathers used to make,
for a defense against the Indians. There is a

broad entrance to it, and, when all is in readiness, the beaters go out into the jungle, with the white hunters, to round up the elephants. A number of tame pachyderms are taken along to pursuade the wild ones to follow.

Gradually the elephants are gathered together in a large body, and gently driven toward the stockade. The tame elephants go in first, and the others follow. Then the entrance is closed, and all that remains to be done is to tame the wild beasts, a no very easy task.

"Are you all ready?" asked Ned, after a bit, as he saw Tom come forward with the camera.

"Yes, I'm loaded for some more excitement. You can put me right over the stockade now, Ned, and when we see the herd coming back I'll go down, and take some views from the ground."

"I think they've got 'em turned," said Mr. Damon. "It sounds as if they were coming back this way."

A moment later they had a glimpse of the herd down below. It was true that the hunters had succeeded in stopping the stampede, and once more the huge beasts were going in the right direction.

"There's a good place to make a landing," suggested Tom, as he saw a comparatively clear place in the jungle. "It's near the stockade, and, in case of danger, I can make a quick get-away."

"What kind of danger are you looking for?" asked Ned, as he shifted the deflecting rudder.

"Oh, one of the beasts might take a notion to chase me."

The landing was made, and Tom, taking Ned and Mr. Nestor with him, and leaving the others to manage the airship in case a quick flight would be necessary, made his way along a jungle trail to the entrance to the stockade. He carried his camera with him, for it was not heavy.

On came the elephants, frightened by the shouts and cries of the beaters, and the firing of guns. The young inventor took his place near the stockade entrance, and, as the elephants advanced through the forest, tearing up trees and bushes, Tom got some good pictures of them.

Suddenly the advance of the brutes was checked, and the foremost of them raised their trunks, trumpeted in anger, and were about to turn back again.

"Get away from that bloomin' gate!" shouted a hunter to Tom. "You're scaring them as bad as your airship did."

"Yes, they won't go in with you there!" added another man.

Tom slipped around the corner of the stockade, out of sight, and from that vantage point he took scores of pictures, as the tame animals led the wild ones into the fenced enclosure. Then began another wild scene as the gate was closed.

The terrified animals rushed about, trying in vain to find a way of escape. Tom managed to climb up on top of the logs, and got some splendid pictures. But this was nearly his undoing. For, just as the last elephant rushed in, a big bull charged against the stockade, and jarred Tom so that he was on the point of falling. His one thought was about his camera, and he looked to see if he could drop it on the soft grass, so it would not be damaged.

He saw Koku standing below him, the giant having slipped out of the airship, to see the beasts at closer range.

"Catch this, Koku!" cried Tom, tossing the big man his precious camera, and the giant caught it safely. But Tom's troubles were not over. A moment later, as the huge elephant again rammed the fence, Tom fell off, but fortunately outside. Then the large beast, seeing a small opening in the gate that was not yet entirely closed, made for it. A moment later he was rushing straight at Tom, who was somewhat stunned by his fall, though it was not a severe one.

"Look out!" yelled Ned.

"Take a tree, Tom!" cried Mr. Nestor.

The elephant paid no attention to any one but Tom, whom he semed to think had caused all his trouble. The young inventor dashed to one side, and then started to run toward the airship, for which Ned and Mr. Nestor were already making. The elephant hunters at last succeeded in closing the gate, blocking the chance of any more animals to escape.

"Run, Tom! Run!" yelled Ned, and Tom ran as he had never run before. The elephant was close after him though, crashing through the jungle. Tom could see the airship just ahead of him.

Suddenly he felt something grasp him from behind. He thought surely it was the elephant's trunk, but a quick glance over his shoulder showed him the friendly face of Koku, the giant.

"Me run for you," said Koku, as he caught Tom up under one arm, and, carrying the camera under the other, he set off at top speed. Now Koku could run well at times, and this time he did. He easily outdistanced the elephant, and, a little later, he set Tom down on the deck of the airship, with the camera beside him. Then Ned and Mr. Nestor came up panting, having run to one side.

"Quick!" cried Tom. "We must get away before the elephant charges the *Flyer*."

"He has stopped," shouted Mr. Nestor, and it was indeed so. The big beast, seeing again the strange craft that had frightened him before, stood still for a moment, and then plunged off into the jungle, trumpeting with rage.

"Safe!" gasped Tom, as he looked at his camera to see if it had been damaged. It seemed all right.

"Bless my latch key!" cried Mr. Damon. "This moving picture business isn't the most peaceful one in the world."

"No, it has plenty of perils," agreed Mr. Nestor.

"Come on, let's get out of here while we have the chance," suggested Tom. "There may be another herd upon us before we know it."

The airship was soon ascending, and Tom and his companions could look down and see the tame elephants in the stockade trying to calm the wild ones. Then the scene faded from sight.

"Well, if these pictures come out all right I'll have some fine ones," exclaimed Tom as he carried his camera to the room where he kept the films. "I fancy an elephant drive and stampede are novelties in this line."

"Indeed they are," agreed Mr. Nestor. "Mr.

Period made no mistake when he picked you out, Tom, for this work. What are you going to try for next?"

"I'd like to get some lion and tiger pictures," said the young inventor. "I understand this is a good district for that. As soon as those elephants get quieted down, I'm going back to the stockade and have a talk with the hunters."

This he did, circling about in the airship until nearly evening. When they again approached the stockade all was quiet, and they came to earth. A native showed them where the white hunters had their headquarters, in some bungalows, and Tom and his party were made welcome. They apologized for frightening the big beasts, and the hunters accepted their excuses.

"As long as we got 'em, it's all right," said the head man, "though for awhile, I didn't like your bloomin' machine." Tom entertained the hunters aboard his craft, at which they marvelled much, and they gave him all the information they had about the lions and tigers in the vicinity.

"You won't find lions and tigers in herds, like elephants though," said the head hunter. "And you may have to photograph 'em at night, as then is when they come out to hunt, and drink."

"Well, I can take pictures at night," said Tom, as he showed his camera apparatus.

The next day, in the airship, they left for another district, where, so the natives reported, several lions had been seen of late. They had done much damage, too, carrying off the native cattle, and killing several Indians.

For nearly a week Tom circled about in his airship, keeping a sharp lookout down below for a sign of lions that he might photograph them. But he saw none, though he did get some pictures of a herd of Indian deer that were well worth his trouble.

"I think I'll have to try for a night photograph," decided Tom at last. "I'll locate a spring where wild beasts are in the habit of coming, set the camera with the light going, and leave it there."

"But will the lions come up if they see the light?" asked Ned.

"I think so," replied his chum. "I'll take a chance, anyhow. If that doesn't work then I'll hide near by, and see what happens."

"Bless my cartridge belt!" cried Mr. Damon. "You don't mean that; do you Tom?"

"Of course. Come to think of it, I'm not going to leave my camera out there for a lion to jump on, and break. As soon as I get a series of pictures I'll bring it back to the ship, I think."

By inquiry among the natives they learned the

location of a spring where, it was said, lions were in the habit of coming nightly to drink.

"That's the place I want!" cried Tom.

Accordingly the airship was headed for it, and one evening it came gently to earth in a little clearing on the edge of the jungle, while Koku, as was his habit, got supper.

After the meal Tom and Ned set the camera, and then, picking out a good spot nearby, they hid themselves to wait for what might happen. The lens was focused on the spring, and the powerful electric light set going. It glowed brightly, and our hero thought it might have the effect of keeping the beasts away, but Tom figured that, after they had looked at it for a while, and seen that it did not harm them, they would lose their suspicions, and come within range of his machine.

"The camera will do the rest," he said. In order not to waste films uselessly Tom arranged a long electric wire, running it from the camera to where he and Ned were hid. By pressing a button he could start or stop the camera any time he wished, and, as he had a view of the spring from his vantage point, he could have the apparatus begin taking pictures as soon as there was some animal within focus.

"Well, I'm getting stiff," said Ned, after an

hour or so had passed in silent darkness, the only light being the distant one on the camera.

"So am I," said Tom.

"I don't believe anything will come to-night," went on his chum. "Let's go back and——"

He stopped suddenly, for there was a crackling in the underbrush, and the next moment the jungle vibrated to the mighty roar of a lion.

"He's coming!" hoarsely whispered Tom.

Both lads glanced through the trees toward the camera, and, in the light, they saw a magnificent, tawny beast standing on the edge of the spring. Once more he roared, as if in defiance, and then, as if deciding that the light was not harmful, he stooped to lap up the water

Hardly had he done so than there was another roar, and a moment later a second lion leaped from the dense jungle into the clearing about the spring. The two monarchs of the forest stood there in the glare of the light, and Tom excitedly pressed the button that started the shutter to working, and the film to moving back of the lens.

There was a slight clicking sound in the camera, and the lions turned startedly. Then both growled again, and the next instant they sprang at each other, roaring mightily.

"A fight!" cried Tom. "A lion fight, and right

in front of my camera! It couldn't be better. This is great! This *will* be a film."

"Quiet!" begged Ned. "They'll hear you, and come for us. I don't want to be chewed up!"

"No danger of them hearing me!" cried Tom. and he had to shout to be heard above the roaring of the two tawny beasts, as they bit and clawed each other, while the camera took picture after picture of them.

CHAPTER XIII

A SHOT IN TIME

"Tom, did you ever see anything like it in your life?"

"I never did, Ned! It's wonderful! fearful! And to think that we are here watching it, and that thousands of people will see the same thing thrown on a screen. Oh, look at the big one. The small lion has him down!"

The two lads, much thrilled, crouched down behind a screen of bushes, watching the midnight fight between the lions. On the airship, not far distant, there was no little alarm, for those left behind heard the terrific roars, and feared Tom and Ned might be in some danger. But the lions were too much occupied with their battle, to pay any attention to anything else, and no other wild beasts were likely to come to the spring while the two "kings" were at each other.

It was a magnificent, but terrible battle. The big cats bit and tore at each other, using their terrific claws and their powerful paws, one stroke of which is said to be sufficient to break a bullock's back. Sometimes they would roll out of the focus of the camera, and, at such times, Tom wished he was at the machine to swing the lens around, but he knew it would be dangerous to move. Then the beasts would roll back into the rays of light again, and more pictures of them would be taken.

"I guess the small one is going to win!" said Tom, after the two lions had fought for ten minutes, and the bigger one had been down several times.

"He's younger," agreed Ned, "and I guess the other one has had his share of fights. Maybe this is a battle to see which one is to rule this part of the jungle."

"I guess so," spoke the young inventor, as he pressed the button to stop the camera, as the lions rolled out of focus. "Oh, look!" he cried a moment later, as the animals again rolled into view. Tom started the camera once more. "This is near the end," he said.

The small lion had, by a sudden spring, landed on the back of his rival. There was a terrific struggle, and the older beast went down, the younger one clawing him terribly. Then, so quickly did it happen that the boys could not take in all the details, the older lion rolled over and over, and rid himself of his antagonist. Quickly he got to his feet, while the smaller lion did the same. They stood for a moment eyeing each other, their tails twitching, the hair on their backs bristling, and all the while they uttered frightful roars.

An instant later the larger beast sprang toward his rival. One terrible paw was upraised. The small lion tried to dodge, but was not quick enough. Down came the paw with terrific force, and the boys could hear the back bone snap. Then, clawing his antagonist terribly, as he lay disabled, the older lion, with a roar of triumph, lapped up water, and sprang off through the jungle, leaving his dying rival beside the spring.

"That's the end," cried Tom, as the small lion died, and the young inventor pressed the button stopping his camera. There was a rustle in the leaves back of Tom and Ned, and they sprang up in alarm, but they need not have feared, for it was only Koku, the giant, who, with a portable electrical torch, had come to see how they had fared.

"Mr. Tom all right?" asked the big man, anxiously.

"Yes, and I got some fine pictures. You can carry the camera back now, Koku. I think that roll of film is pretty well filled."

The three of them looked at the body of the dead lion, before they went back to the airship. I have called him "small," but, in reality, the beast was small only in comparison with his rival, who was a tremendous lion in size. I might add that of all the pictures Tom took, few were more highly prized than that reel of the lion fight.

"Bless my bear cage!" cried Mr. Damon, as Tom came back, "you certainly have nerve, my boy."

"You have to, in this business," agreed Tom with a laugh. "I never did this before, and I don't know that I would want it for a steady position, but it's exciting for a change."

They remained near the "lion spring" as they called it all night, and in the morning, after Koku had served a tasty breakfast, Tom headed the airship for a district where it was said there were many antelope, and buffaloes, also zebus.

"I don't want to get *all* exciting pictures," our hero said to Mr. Nestor. "I think that films showing wild animals at play, or quietly feeding, will be good."

"I'm sure they will," said Mary's father. "Get some peaceful scenes, by all means."

They sailed on for several days, taking a number of pictures from the airship, when they passed over a part of the country where the view was magnificent, and finally, stopping at a good sized village they learned that, about ten miles out, was a district where antelope abounded.

"We'll go there," decided Tom, "and I'll take the camera around with me on a sort of walking trip. In that way I'll get a variety of views, and I can make a good film."

This plan was followed out. The airship came to rest in a beautiful green valley, and Ned and Tom, with Mr. Damon, who begged to be taken along, started off.

"You can follow me in about half an hour, Koku," said Tom, "and carry the camera back. I guess you can easily pick up our trail."

"Oh, sure," replied the giant. Indeed, to one who had lived in the forest, as he had all his life, before Tom found him, it was no difficult matter to follow a trail, such as the three friends would leave.

Tom found signs that showed him where the antelopes were in the habit of passing, and, with Ned and Mr. Damon, stationed himself in a secluded spot.

He had not long to wait before a herd of deer came past. Tom took many pictures of the graceful creatures, for it was daylight now, and he needed no light. Consequently there was nothing to alarm the herd.

After having made several films of the antelope, Tom and his two companions went farther on. They were fortunate enough to find a place that seemed to be a regular playground of the deer. There was a large herd there, and, getting as near as he dared, Tom focused his camera, and began taking pictures.

"It's as good as a play," whispered Mr. Damon, as he and Ned watched the creatures, for they had to speak quietly. The camera made scarcely any noise. "I'm glad I came on this trip."

"So am I," said Ned. "Look, Tom, see the mother deer all together, and the fawns near them. It's just as if it was a kindergarten meeting."

"I see," whispered Tom. "I'm getting a picture of that."

For some little time longer Tom photographed the deer, and then, suddenly, the timid creatures all at once lifted up their heads, and darted off. Tom and Ned, wondering what had startled them, looked across the glade just in time to see a big tiger leap out of the tall grass. The striped animal had been stalking the antelope, but they had scented him just in time.

"Get him, Tom," urged Ned, and the young inventor did so, securing several fine views before the tiger bounded into the grass again, and took after his prey.

"Bless my china teacup! What's that!" suddenly cried Mr. Damon. As he spoke there was a crashing in the bushes and, an instant later a two-horned rhinoceros sprang into view, charging straight for the group.

"Look out!" yelled Ned.

"Bless my——" began Mr. Damon, but he did not finish, for, in starting to run his foot caught in the grass, and he went down heavily.

Tom leaped to one side, holding his camera so as not to damage it. But he stumbled over Mr. Damon, and went down.

With a "wuff" of rage the clumsy beast, came on, moving more rapidly than Tom had any idea he was capable of. Hampered by his camera our hero could not arise. The rhinoceros was almost upon him, and Ned, catching up a club, was just going to make a rush to the rescue, when the brute seemed suddenly to crumple up. It fell down in a heap, not five feet from where Tom and Mr. Damon lay.

"Good!" cried Ned. "He's dead. Shot through the heart! Who did it?"

"I did," answered Koku quietly, stepping out of the bushes, with one of Tom's Swift's electric rifles in his hand.

CHAPTER XIV

IN A GREAT GALE

Tom Swift rose slowly to his feet, carefully setting his camera down, after making sure that it was not injured. Then he looked at the huge beast which lay dead in front of him, and, going over to the giant he held out his hand to him.

"Koku, you saved my life," spoke Tom. "Probably the life of Mr. Damon also. I can't begin to thank you. It isn't the first time you've done it, either. But I want to say that you can have anything you want, that I've got."

"Me like this gun pretty much," said the giant simply.

"Then it's yours!" exclaimed Tom. "And you're the only one, except myself, who has ever owned one." Tom's wonderful electric rifle, of which I have told you in the book bearing that name, was one of his most cherished inventions.

He guarded jealously the secret of how it worked, and never sold or gave one away, for fear that unscrupulous men might learn how to make them, and so cause fearful havoc. For the rifle was a terrible weapon. Koku seemed to appreciate the honor done him, as he handled the gun, and looked from it to the dead rhinoceros.

"Bless my blank cartridge!" exclaimed Mr. Damon, as he also got up and came to examine the dead beast. It was the first thing he had said since the animal had rushed at him, and he had not moved after he fell down. He had seemingly been in a daze, but when the others heard him use one of his favorite expressions they knew that he was all right again. "Bless my hat!" went on the odd man. "What happened, Tom? Is that beast really dead? How did Koku come to arrive in time?"

"I guess he's dead all right," said Tom, giving the rhinoceros a kick. "But I don't know how Koku happened to arrive in the nick of time, and with the gun, too."

"I think maybe I see something to shoot when I come after you, like you tell me to do," spoke the giant. "I follow your trail, but I see nothing to shoot until I come here. Then I see that animal run for you, and I shoot."

"And a good thing you did, too," put in Ned. "Well let's go back. My nerves are on edge, and I want to sit quiet for a while."

"Take the camera, Koku," ordered Tom, "and I'll carry the electric rifle—*your* rifle, now," he

added, and the giant grinned in delight. They
reached the airship without further incident, and,
after a cup of tea, Tom took out the exposed
films and put a fresh roll in his camera, ready for
whatever new might happen.

"Where is your next stopping place, Tom?"
asked Ned, as they sat in the main room of the
airship that evening, talking over the events of
the day. They had decided to stay all night anchored on the ground, and start off in the morning.

"I hardly know, answered the young inventor.
"I am going to set the camera to-night, near a
small spring I saw, to get some pictures of deer
coming to drink. I may get a picture of a lion
or a tiger attacking them. If I could it would
be another fine film. To-morrow I think we will
start for Switzerland. But now I'm going to
get the camera ready for a night exposure."

"Bless my check book!" cried Mr. Damon.
"You don't mean to say that you are going to
stay out at a spring again, Tom, and run the
chance of a tiger getting you."

"No, I'm merely going to set the camera, at-
tach the light and let it work automatically this
time. I've put in an extra long roll of film, for
I'm going to keep it going for a long while,
and part of the time there may be no animals

there to take pictures of. No, I'm not going to sit out to-night. I'm too tired. I'll conceal the camera in the bushes so it won't be damaged if there's a fight. Then, as I said, we'll start for Switzerland to-morrow."

"Switzerland!" cried Ned. "What in the world do you want to go make a big jump like that for? And what do you expect to get in that mountain land?"

"I'm going to try for a picture of an avalanche," said Tom. "Mr. Period wants one, if I can get it. It is quite a jump, but then we'll be flying over civilized countries most of the time, and if any accident happens we can go down and easily make repairs. We can also get gasolene for the motor, though I have quite a supply in the tanks, and perhaps enough for the entire trip. At the same time we won't take any chances. So we'll be off for Switzerland in the morning."

"I think some avalanche pictures will be great, if you can get them," remarked Mr. Nestor. "But, Tom, you know those big slides of ice, snow and earth aren't made to order."

"Oh, I know," agreed the young inventor with a smile. "I'll just have to take my chances, and wait until one happens."

"Bless my insurance policy!" exclaimed Mr.

Damon. "And when it *does* happen, Tom, are you going to stand in front of it, and snap-shot it?"

"Indeed I'm not. This business is risky and dangerous enough, without looking for trouble. I'm going to the mountain region, and hover around in the air, until we see an avalanche 'happen' if that is the right word. Then I'll focus the camera on it, and the films and machinery will do the rest."

"Oh, that's different," remarked the odd man, with an air of relief.

Tom and Ned soon had the camera set near the spring and then, everyone being tired with the day's work and excitement, they retired. In the morning there were signs around the spring that many animals had been there in the night. There were also marks as if there had been a fight, but of course what sort, or how desperate, no one could say.

"If anything happened the camera got it, I'm sure of that much," remarked Tom, as he brought in the apparatus. "I'm not going to develope the roll, for I don't want to take the time now.' I guess we must have something, anyhow."

"If there isn't it won't so much matter for you have plenty of other good views," said Mr. Nestor.

I will not go into details of the long trip to Switzerland, where, amid the mountains of that country, Tom hoped to get the view he wanted.

Sufficient to say that the airship made good time after leaving India. Sometimes Tom sent the craft low down, in order to get views, and again, it would be above the clouds.

"Well, another day will bring us there," said Tom one evening, as he was loading the camera with a fresh roll of films. "Then we'll have to be on the lookout for an avalanche."

"Yes, we're making pretty good time," remarked Ned, as he looked at the speed gage. "I didn't know you had the motor working so fast, Tom."

"I haven't," was the young inventor's answer, as he looked up in surprise. "Why, we are going quite fast! It's the wind, Ned. It's right with us, and it's carrying us along."

Tom arose and went to the anemometer, or wind-registering instrument. He gave a low whistle, half of alarm.

"Fifty miles an hour she's blowing now," he said. "It came on suddenly, too, for a little while ago it was only ten."

"Is there any danger?" asked Mr. Nestor, for he was not very familiar with airship perils.

"Well, we've been in big blows before, and we

generally came out all right," returned Tom. "Still, I don't like this. Why she went up five points since I've been looking at it!" and he pointed to the needle of the gage, which now registered fifty-five miles an hour.

"Bless my appendix!" gasped Mr. Damon. "It's a hurricane Tom!"

"Something like that," put in Ned, in a low voice.

With a suddenness that was startling, the wind increased in violence still more. Tom ran to the pilot house.

"What are you going to do?" Ned called.

"See if we can't go down a bit," was Tom's answer. "I don't like this. It may be calmer below. We're up too high as it is."

He tried to throw over the lever controlling the deflecting rudder, which would send the *Flyer* down, but he could not move it.

"Give me a hand!" he called to Ned, but even the strength of the two lads was not sufficient to shift it.

"Call Koku!" gasped Tom. "If anybody can budge it the giant can!"

Meanwhile the airship was being carried onward in the grip of a mighty wind, so strong that its pressure on the surface of the deflecting rudder prevented it from being shifted.

CHAPTER XV

SNAPPING AN AVALANCHE

"BLESS my thermometer!" gasped Mr. Damon. "This is terrible!" The airship was plunging and swaying about in the awful gale. "Can't something be done, Tom?"

"What has happened?" cried Mr. Nestor. "We were on a level keel before. What is it?"

"It's the automatic balancing rudder!" answered Tom. "Something has happened to it. The wind may have broken it! Come on, Ned!" and he led the way to the engine room.

"What are you going to do? Don't you want Koku to shift the deflecting rudder? Here he is," Ned added, as the giant came forward, in response to a signal bell that Tom's chum had rung.

"It's too late to try the deflecting rudder!" cried Tom. "I must see what is the matter with our balancer." As he spoke the ship gave a terrific plunge, and the occupants were thrown sideways. The next moment it was on a level keel again, scudding along with the gale, but there was no telling when the craft would again nearly capsize.

Tom looked at the mechanism controlling the equalizing and equilibrium rudder. It was out of order, and he guessed that the terrific wind was responsible for it.

"What can we do?" cried Ned, as the airship nearly rolled over. "Can't we do anything, Tom?"

"Yes. I'm going to try. Keep calm now. We may come out all right. This is the worst blow we've been in since we were in Russia. Start the gas machine full blast. I want all the vapor I can get."

As I have explained the *Flyer* was a combined dirigible balloon and aeroplane. It could be used as either, or both, in combination. At present the gas bag was not fully inflated, and Tom had been sending his craft along as an aeroplane.

"What are you going to do?" cried Ned, as he pulled over the lever that set the gas generating machine in operation.

"I'm going up as high as I can go!" cried Tom. "If we can't go down we must go up. I'll get *above* the hurricane instead of *below* it. Give me all the gas you can, Ned!"

The vapor hissed as it rushed into the big bag

overhead. Tom carried aboard his craft the chemicals needed to generate the powerful lifting gas,
of which he alone had the secret. It was more
powerful than hydrogen, and simple to make.
The balloon of the *Flyer* was now being dis-
tended.

Meanwhile Tom, with Koku, Mr. Damon and
Mr. Nestor to help him, worked over the deflecting rudder, and also on the equilibrium mechanism. But they could not get either to operate.

Ned stood by the gas machine, and worked it
to the limit. But even with all that energy, so
powerful was the wind, that the *Flyer* rose slowly, the gale actually holding her down as a water-
logged craft is held below the waves. Ordinarily,
with the gas machine set at its limit the craft
would have shot up rapidly.

At times the airship would skim along on the
level, and again it would be pitched and tossed
about, until it was all the occupants could do to
keep their feet. Mr. Damon was continually
blessing everything he could remember.

"Now she's going!" suddenly cried Ned, as he
looked at the dials registering the pressure of
the gas, and showing the height of the airship
above the earth.

"Going how?" gasped Tom, as he looked over

from where he was working at the equilibrium apparatus. "Going down?"

"Going up!" shouted Ned. "I guess we'll be all right soon!"

It was true. Now that the bag was filled with the powerful lifting gas, under pressure, the *Flyer* was beginning to get out of the dangerous predicament into which the gale had blown her, Up and up she went, and every foot she climbed the power of the wind became less.

"Maybe it all hapened for the best," said Tom, as he noted the height gage. "If we had gone down, the wind might have been worse nearer the earth."

Later they learned that this was so. The most destructive wind storm ever known swept across the southern part of Europe, over which they were flying that night, and, had the airship gone down, she would probably have been destroyed. But, going up, she got above the wind-strata. Up and up she climbed, until, when three miles above the earth, she was in a calm zone. It was rather hard to breathe at this height, and Tom set the oxygen apparatus at work.

This created in the interior of the craft an atmosphere almost like that on the earth, and the travelers were made more at their ease. Getting out of the terrible wind pressure made it possible to work the deflecting rudder, though Tom had no idea of going down, as long as the blow lasted.

"We'll just sail along at this height until morning," he said, "and by then the gale may be over, or we may be beyond the zone of it. Start the propellers, Ned. I think I can manage to repair the equilibrium rudder now."

The propellers, which gave the forward motion to the airship, had been stopped when it was found that the wind was carying her along, but they were now put in motion again, sending the *Flyer* forward. In a short time Tom had the equilibrium machine in order, and matters were now normal again.

"But that was a strenuous time while it lasted," remarked the young inventor, as he sat down.

"It sure was," agreed Ned.

"Bless my pen wiper!" cried Mr. Damon. "That was one of the few times when I wish I'd never come with you, Tom Swift," and everyone laughed at that.

The *Flyer* was now out of danger, going along high in the air through the night, while the gale raged below her. At Tom's suggestion, Koku got a lunch ready, for they were all tired with their labors, and somewhat nervous from the danger and excitement.

"And now for sleep!" exclaimed Tom, as he pushed back his plate. "Ned, set the automatic steering gear, and we'll see where we bring up by morning."

An examination, through a powerful telescope in the bright light of morning, showed the travelers that they were over the outskirts of a large city, which, later, they learned was Rome, Italy.

"We've made a good trip," said Tom. "The gale had us worried, but it sent us along at a lively clip. Now for Switzerland, and the avalanches!"

They made a landing at a village just outside the "Holy City," as Rome is often called, and renewed their supply of gasolene. Naturally they attracted a crowd of curious persons, many of whom had never seen an airship before. Certainly few of them had ever seen one like Tom Swift's.

The next day found them hovering over the Alps, where Tom hoped to be able to get the pictures of snow slides. They went down to earth at a town near one of the big mountain ranges, and there made inquiries as to where would be the best location to look for big avalanches. If they went but a few miles to the north, they were told, they would be in the desired region, and they departed for that vicinity.

"And now we've just got to take our time, and wait for an avalanche to happen," remarked Tom, as they were flying along over the mountain ranges. "As Mr. Damon said, these things aren't made to order. They just happen."

For three days they sailed in and out over the great snow-covered peaks of the Alps. They did not go high up, for they wanted to be near earth when an avalanche would occur, so that near-view pictures could be secured. Occasionally they saw parties of mountain climbers ascending some celebrated peak, and for want of something better to photograph, Tom "snapped" the tourists.

"Well, I guess they're all out of avalanches this season," remarked Ned one afternoon, when they had circled back and forth over a mountain where, so it was said, the big snow slides were frequent.

"It does seem so," agreed Tom. "Still, we're in no hurry. It is easier to be up here, than it is walking around in a jungle, not knowing what minute a tiger may jump out at you."

"Bless my rubbers, yes!" agreed Mr. Damon.

The sky was covered with lowering clouds, and there were occasionally flurries of snow.

Tom's airship was well above the snow line on the mountains. The young inventor and Ned sat in the pilot house, taking observations through a spyglass of the mountain chain below them.

Suddenly Ned, who had the glass focused on a mighty peak, cried out:

"There she is, Tom!"

"What?"

"The avalanche! The snow is beginning to slide down the mountain! Say, it's going to be a big one, too. Got your camera ready?"

"Sure! I've had it ready for the last three days. Put me over there, Ned. You look after the airship, and I'll take the pictures!"

Tom sprang to get his apparatus, while his chum hurried to the levers, wheels and handles that controlled the *Flyer*. As they approached the avalanche they could see the great mass of ice, snow, big stones, and earth sliding down the mountain side, carrying tall trees with it.

"This is just what I wanted!" cried Tom, as ne set his camera working. "Put me closer, Ned."

Ned obeyed, and the airship was now hovering directly over the avalanche, and right in its path. The big landslide, as it would have been called in this country, met no village in its path, fortunately, or it would have wiped it out completely. It

was in a wild and desolate region that it occurred.

"I want to get a real close view!" cried Tom,
as he got some pictures showing a whole grove
of giant trees uprooted and carried off. "Get
closer Ned, and——"

Tom was interrupted by a cry of alarm from
his chum.

"We're falling!" yelled Ned. "Something has
gone wrong. We're going down into the avalanche!"

CHAPTER XVI

TELEGRAPH ORDERS

THERE was confusion aboard the airship. Tom, hearing Ned's cry, left his camera, to rush to the engine room, but not before he had set the picture apparatus to working automatically. Mr. Damon, Mr. Nestor and Koku, alarmed by Ned's cries, ran back from the forward part of the craft, where they had been watching the mighty mass of ice and earth as it rushed down the side of the mountain.

"What's wrong, Ned?" cried Tom excitedly.

"I don't know! The propellers have stopped! We were running as an aeroplane you know. Now we're going down!"

"Bless my suspenders!" shouted Mr. Damon. "If we land in the midst of that conglomeration of ice it will be the end of us."

"But we're not going to land there!" cried Tom.

"How are you going to stop it?" demanded Mr. Nestor.

"By the gas machine!" answered Tom. "That will stop us from falling. Start it up, Ned!"

"That's right! I always forget about that! I'll have it going in a second!"

"Less than a second," called Tom, as he saw how near to the mighty, rushing avalanche they were coming.

Ned worked rapidly, and in a very short time the downward course of the airship was checked. It floated easily above the rushing flood of ice and earth, and Tom, seeing that his craft, and those on it, were safe, hurried back to his camera. Meanwhile the machine had automatically been taking pictures, but now with the young inventor to manage it, better results would be obtained.

Tom aimed it here and there, at the most spectacular parts of the avalanche. The others gathered around him, after Ned had made an inspection, and found that a broken electrical wire had caused the propellers to stop. This was soon repaired and then, as they were hanging in the air like a balloon, Tom took picture after picture of the wonderful sight below them. Forest after forest was demolished.

"This will be a great film!" Tom shouted to Ned, as the latter informed him that the machinery was all right again. "Send me up a little. I want to get a view from the top, looking down."

His chum made the necessary adjustments to the mechanism and then, there being nothing more to slide down the mountainside the avalanche was ended. But what a mass of wreck and ruin there was! It was as if a mighty earthquake had torn the mountain asunder.

"It's a good thing it wasn't on a side of the mountain where people lived," commented Ned, as the airship rose high toward the clouds. "If it had been, there'd be nothing left of 'em. What hair-raising stunt are you going to try next, Tom?"

"I don't know. I expect to hear from Mr. Period soon."

"Hear from Mr. Period?" exclaimed Mr. Nestor. "How are you going to do that, Tom?"

"He said he would telegraph me at Berne, Switzerland, at a certain date, as he knew I was coming to the Alps to try for some avalanche pictures. It's two or three days yet, before I can expect the telegram, which of course will have to come part way by cable. In the meanwhile, I think we'll take a little rest, and a vacation. I want to give the airship an overhauling, and look to my camera. There's no telling what Mr. Period may want next."

"Then he didn't make out your programme

completely before you started?" asked **Mr.** Nestor.

"No, he said he'd communicate with me from time to time. He is in touch with what is going 'on in the world, you know, and if he hears of anything exciting at any place, I'm to go there at once. You see he wants the most sensational films he can get."

"Yes, our company is out to give the best pictures we can secure," spoke Mary's father, "and I think we are lucky to have Tom Swift working for us. We already have films that no other concern can get. And we need them."

"I wonder what became of those men who started to make so much trouble for you, Tom?" asked Mr. Damon.

"Well, they seem to have disappeared," replied our hero. "Of course they may be after me any day now, but for the time being, I've thrown them off my track."

"So then you don't know where you're going next?" asked Ned.

"No, it may be to Japan, or to the North Pole. Well, I'm ready for anything. We've got plenty of gasolene, and the *Flyer* can certainly go," said Tom.

They went down to earth in a quiet spot, just outside of a little village, and there they remained three days, to the no small wonder of the inhabitants. Tom wanted to see if his camera was working properly. So he developed some of the avalanche pictures, and found them excellent. The rest of the time was spent in making some needed repairs to the airship, while the young inventor overhauled his Wizard machine, that he found needed a few adjustments.

Their arrival in Berne created quite a sensation, but they were used to that. Tom anchored his airship just outside the city, and, accompanied by Ned, made his way to the teleghaph office. Some of the officials there could speak English, though not very well.

"I am expecting a message," said Tom.

"Yes? Who for?" asked the clerk.

"Tom Swift. It will be from America."

As Tom said this he observed a man sitting in the corner of the office get up hurriedly and go out. All at once his suspicions were aroused. He thought of the attempts that had been made to get his Wizard Camera away from him.

"Who was that man?" he quickly asked the agent.

"Him? Oh, he, too, is expecting a message from America. He has been here some time."

"Why did he go out so quickly?" Ned wanted to know.

"Why, I can not tell. He is an Englishman. They do strange things."

"My telegram? Is it here?" asked Tom impatiently. He wanted to get whatever word there was from Mr. Period, and be on his way to whatever destination the picture man might select. Perhaps, after all, his suspicions, against the man who had so suddenly left, were unfounded.

"Yes, there is a cablegram here for you, Monsieur Swift," said the man, who was French. "There are charges on it, however."

"Pay 'em, Ned, while I see what this is," directed the young inventor, as he tore open the envelope.

"Whew!" he whistled a moment later. "This *is* going some."

"Where to now?" asked Ned. "The North Pole?"

"No, just the opposite. Mr. Period wants me to go to Africa—the Congo Free State. There's an uprising among the natives there, and he wants some war pictures. Well, I guess I'll have to go."

As Tom spoke he looked toward the door of the telegraph office, and he saw the man, who had so hurriedly gone out a few moments before, looking in at him.

CHAPTER XVII

SUSPICIOUS STRANGERS

"Off to Africa; eh?" remarked Ned, as Tom put the envelope in his pocket. "That's another long jump. But I guess the *Flyer* can do it, Tom"

"Yes, I think so. I say Ned, not so loud," and Tom, who had hurried to the side of his chum, whispered the last words.

"What's up?" inquired Ned quickly. "Anything wrong?"

"I don't know. But I think we are being watched. Did you notice that fellow who was in here a minute ago, when I asked for a telegram?"

"Yes, what about him?"

"Well, he's looking in the door now I think. Don't turn round. Just look up into that mirror on the wall, and you can see his reflection."

"I understand," whispered Ned, as he turned his gaze toward the mirror in question, a large one, with advertisements around the frame. "I see him," he went on. "There's some one with him."

"That's what I thought," replied Tom. "Take a good look. Whom do you think the other chap is?"

Ned looked long and earnestly. By means of the mirror, he could see, perfectly plain, two men standing just outside the door of the telegraph office. The portal was only partly open. Ned drew an old letter from his pocket, and pretended to be showing it to Tom. But, all the while he was gazing earnestly at the two men. Suddenly one of them moved, giving Tom's chum a better view of his face.

"By Jove, Tom!" the lad exclaimed in a tense whisper. "If it isn't that Eckert fellow I'm a cow."

"That's what I thought," spoke Tom coolly. "Not that you're a cow, Ned, but I believe that this man is one of the moving picture partners, who are rivals of Mr. Period. I wasn't quite sure myself after the first glance I had of him, so I wanted you to take a look. Do you know the other chap—the one who ran out when I asked for my telegram?"

"No, I've never seen him before as far as I know."

"Same here. Come on."

"What are you going to do?"

"Go back to the airship, and tell Mr. Nestor.

As one of the directors in the concern I'm working for. I want his advice."

"Good idea," replied Ned, and they turned to leave the office. The spying stranger, and William Eckert, were not in sight when the two lads came out.

"They got away mighty quick," remarked Tom, as he looked up and down the street.

"Yes, they probably saw us turn to come out, and made a quick get-away. They might be in any one of these places along here," for the street, on either side of the telegraph office, contained a number of hotels, with doors opening on the sidewalk.

"They must be on your trail yet," decided Mr. Nestor when Tom, reaching the anchored airship, told what had happened. "Well, my advice is to go to Africa as soon as we can. In that way we'll leave them behind, and they won't have any chance to get your camera."

"But what I can't understand," said Tom, "is how they knew I was coming here. It was just as if that one man had been waiting in the telegraph office for me to appear. I'm sorry, now, that I mentioned to Ned where we were ordered to. But I didn't think."

"They probably knew, anyway," was Mr. Nestor's opinion. "I think this may explain it. The rival concern in New York has been keeping track of Mr. Period's movements. Probably they have a paid spy who may be in his employ. They knew when he sent you a telegram, what it contained, and where it was directed to. Then, of course, they knew you would call here for it. What they did not know was *when* you would come, and so they had to wait. That one spy was on guard, and, as soon as you came, he went and summoned Eckert, who was waiting somewhere in the neighborhood."

"Bless my detective story!" cried Mr. Damon. "What a state of affairs! They ought to be arrested, Tom."

"It would be useless," said Mr. Nestor. "They are probably far enough away by this time. Or else they have put others on Tom's track."

"I'll fight my own battles!" exclaimed the young inventor. "I don't go much on the police in a case like this, especially foreign police. Well, my camera is all right, so far," he went on, as he took a look at it, in the compartment where he kept it. "Some one must always remain near it, after this. But we'll soon start for Africa, to get some pictures of a native battle. I hope it isn't the red pygmies we have to photograph."

"Bless my shoe laces! Don't suggest such a thing," begged Mr. Damon, as he recalled the strenuous times when the dwarfs held the missionaries captive.

It was necessary to lay in some stores and provisions, and for this reason Tom could not at once head the airship for the African jungles. As she remained at anchor, just outside the city, crowds of Swiss people came out to look at the wonderful craft. But Tom and his companions took care that no one got aboard, and they kept a strict lookout for Americans, or Englishmen, thinking perhaps that Mr. Eckert, or the spy, might try to get the camera. However, they did not see them, and a few days after the receipt of the message from Mr. Period, having stocked up, they rose high into the air, and set out to cross the Mediterranean Sea for Africa. Tom laid a route over Tripoli, the Sahara Desert, the French Congo, and so into the Congo Free State. In his telegram, Mr. Period had said that the expected uprising was to take place near Stanley Falls, on the Congo River.

"And supposing it does *not* happen?" asked Mr. Damon. "What if the natives don't fight, Tom? You'll have your trip for nothing, and will run a lot of risk besides."

"It's one of the chances I'm taking," replied the young inventor, and truly, as he thought of it, he realized that the perils of the moving picture business were greater than he had imagined.

Tom hoped to get a quick trip to the Congo, but, as they were sailing over the big desert, there was an accident to the main motor, and the airship suddenly began shooting toward the sands. She was easily brought up, by means of the gas bags, and allowed to settle gently to the ground, in the vicinity of a large oasis. But, when Tom looked at the broken machinery, he said:

"This means a week's delay. It will take that, and longer, to fix it so we can go on."

"Too bad!" exclaimed Mr. Nestor. "The war may be over when we get there. But it can't be helped."

It took Tom and his friends even longer than he had thought to make the repairs. In the meanwhile they camped in the desert place, which was far from being unpleasant. Occasionally a caravan halted there, but, for the most part, they were alone.

"No danger of Eckert, or any of his spies coming here, I guess," said Tom grimly as he blew on a portable forge, to weld two pieces of iron together.

In due time they were again on the wing, and without further incident they were soon in the vicinity of Stanley Falls. They managed to locate a village where there were some American missionaries established. They were friends of Mr. and Mrs. Illington, the missionaries whom Tom had saved from the red pygmies, as told in the "Electric Rifle" volume of this series, and they made our hero and his friends welcome.

"Is it true?" asked Tom, of the missionaries who lived not far from Stanley Falls, "that there is to be a native battle? Or are we too late for it?"

"I am sorry to say, I fear there *will* be fighting among the tribesmen," replied Mr. Janeway, one of the Christian workers. "It has not yet taken place, though."

"Then I'm not too late!" cried Tom, and there was exultation in his voice. "I don't mean to be barbarous," he went on, as he saw that the missionaries looked shocked, "but as long as they *are* going to fight I want to get the pictures."

"Oh, they'll fight all right," spoke Mrs. Janeway. "The poor, ignorant natives here are always ready to fight. This time I think it is about some cattle that one tribe took from another."

"And where will the battle take place?" asked Tom.

"Well, the rumors we have, seem to indicate that the fight will take place about ten miles north of here. We will have notice of it before it starts, as some of the natives, whom we have succeeded in converting, belong to the tribe that is to be attacked. They will be summoned to the defense of their town and then it will be time enough for you to go. Oh, war is a terrible thing! I do not like to talk about it. Tell me how you rescued our friends from the red pygmies," and Tom was obliged to relate that story, which I have told in detail elsewhere.

Several days passed, and Tom and his friends spent a pleasant time in the African village with the missionaries. The airship and camera were in readiness for instant use, and during this period of idleness our hero got several fine films of animal scenes, including a number of night-fights among the beasts at the drinking pools. One tiger battle was especially good, from a photographic standpoint.

One afternoon, a number of native bearers came into the town. They preceded two white men, who were evidently sportsmen, or explorers, and the latter had a well equipped caravan. The strangers sought the advice of the missionaries about where big game might be found, and Tom happened to be at the cottage of Mr. Janeway when the strangers arrived.

The young inventor looked at them critically, as he was introduced to them. Both men spoke with an English accent, one introducing himself as Bruce Montgomery, and the other as Wade Kenneth. Tom decided that they were of the ordinary type of globe-trotting Britishers, until, on his way to his airship, he passed the place where the native bearers had set down the luggage of the Englishmen.

"Whew!" whistled Tom, as he caught sight of a peculiarly shaped box. "See that, Ned?"

"Yes, what is it? A new kind of magazine gun?"

"It's a moving picture camera, or I lose my guess!" whispered Tom. "One of the old fashioned kind. Those men are no more tourists, or after big game, than I am! They're moving picture men, and they're here to get views of that native battle! Ned, we've got to be on our guard. They may be in the pay of that Turbot and Eckert firm, and they may try to do us some harm!"

"That's so!" exclaimed Ned. "We'll keep watch of them, Tom."

As they neared their airship, there came, running down what served as the main village street, an African who showed evidence of having come from afar. As he ran on, he called out something in a strange tongue. Instantly from their huts the other natives swarmed.

"What's up now?" cried Ned.

"Something important, I'll wager," replied Tom. "Ned, you go back to the missionaries' house, and find out what it is. I'm going to stand guard over my camera."

"It's come!" cried Ned a little later, as he hurried into the interior of the airship, where Tom was busy working over a new attachment he intended putting on his picture machine.

"What has?"

"War! That native, whom we saw running in, brought news that the battle would take place day after to-morrow. The enemies of his tribe are on the march, so the African spies say, and he came to summon all the warriors from this town. We've got to get busy!"

"That's so. What about those Enghlishmen?"

"They were talking to the missionaries when the runner came in. They pretended to have no interest in it, but I saw one wink to the other, and then, very soon, they went out, and I saw them talking to their native bearers, while they were busy over that box you said was a picture machine."

"I knew it, Ned! I was sure of it! Those fellows came here to trick us, though how they ever followed our trail I don't know. Probably they came by a fast steamer to the West Coast, and struck inland, while we were delayed on the desert. I don't care if they are only straight out-and-out rivals—and not chaps that are trying to take an unfair advantage. I suppose all the big picture concerns have a tip about this war, and they may have representatives here. I hope we get the best views. Now come on, and give me a hand. We've got our work cut out for us, all right."

"Bless my red cross bandage!" cried Mr. Damon, when he heard the news. "A native fight, eh? That will be something I haven't seen in some time. Will there be any danger, Tom, do you think?"

"Not unless our airship tumbles down between the two African forces," replied our hero, "and I'll take care that it doesn't do that. "We'll be well out of reach of any of their blow guns, or arrows."

"But I understand that many of the tribes have powder weapons," said Mr. Nestor.

"They have," admitted Tom, "but they are 'trader's' rifles, and don't carry far. We won't run any risk from such old-fashioned guns."

"A big fight; eh?" asked Koku when they told him what was before them. "Me like to help."

"Yes, and I guess both sides would give a premium for your services," remarked Tom, as he gazed at his big servant. "But we'll need you with us, Koku."

"Oh, me stay with *you,* Mr. Tom," exclaimed the big man, with a grin.

Somewhat to Tom's surprise the two Englishmen showed no further interest in him and his airship, after the introduction at the missionaries' bungalow.

With the stolidity of their race the Britishers did not show any surprise, as, some time afterward, they strolled down toward Tom's big craft, after supper, and looked it over. Soon they went back to their own camp, and a little later, Koku, who walked toward it, brought word that the Englishmen were packing up.

"They're going to start for the seat of war the first thing in the morning," decided Tom. "Well, we'll get ahead of them. Though we can travel faster than they can, we'll start now, and be on the ground in good season. Besides, I don't like staying all night in the same neighborhood with them. Get ready for a start, Ned."

Tom did not stop to say good-bye to the Englishmen, though he bade farewell to the missionaries, who had been so kind to him. There was much excitement in the native town, for many of the tribesmen were getting ready to depart to help their friends or relatives in the impending battle.

As dusk was falling, the big airship arose, and soon her powerful propellers were sending her across the jungle, toward Stanley Falls in the vicinity of which the battle was expected to take place.

CHAPTER XVIII

THE NATIVE BATTLE

"By Jove, Tom, here they come!"

"From over by that drinking pool?"

"Yes, just as the spies said they would. Wow, what a crowd of the black beggars there are! And some of 'em have regular guns, too. But most of 'em have clubs, bows and arrows, blow guns, or spears."

Tom and Ned were standing on the forward part of the airship, which was moving slowly along, over an open plateau, in the jungle where the native battle was about to take place. Our friends had left the town where the missionaries lived, and had hovered over the jungle, until they saw signs of the coming struggle. They had seen nothing of their English rivals since coming away, but had no doubt but that the Britishers were somewhere in the neighborhood.

The two forces of black men, who had gone to war over a dispute about some cattle, approached each other. There was the beating of tom-toms, and skin drums, and many weird shouts. From their vantage point in the air, Tom and his companions had an excellent view. The Wizard Camera was loaded with a long reel of film, and ready for action.

"Bless my handkerchief!" cried Mr. Damon, as he looked down on the forces that were about to clash. "I never saw anything like this before!"

"I either," admitted Tom. "But, if things go right, I'm going to get some dandy films!"

Nearer and nearer the rival forces advanced. At first they had stared, and shouted in wonder at the sight of the airship, hovering above them, but their anger soon drew their attention to the fighting at hand, and, after useless gestures toward the craft of the air, and after some of them had vainly fired their guns or arrows at it, they paid no more attention, but rushed on with their shouts and cries and amid the beating of their rude drums.

"I think I'll begin to take pictures now," said Tom, as Ned, in charge of the ship, sent it about in a circle, giving a general view of the rival forces. "I'll show a scene of the two crowds getting ready for business, and, later on, when they're actually giving each other cats and dogs, I'll get all the pictures possible."

The camera was started while, safe in the air, those on the *Flyer* watched what went on below them.

Suddenly the forward squads of the two small armies of blacks met. With wild, weird yells they rushed at each other. The air was filled with flying arrows and spears. The sound of the old-fashioned muzzle-loading guns could be heard, and clouds of smoke arose. Tilting his camera, and arranging the newly attached reflecting mirrors so as to give the effect as if a spectator was looking at the battle from in front, instead of from above, Tom Swift took picture after picture.

The fight was now on. With yells of rage and defiance the Africans came together, giving blow for blow. It was a wild meleé, and those on the airship looked on fascinated, though greatly wishing that such horrors could be stopped.

"How about it, Tom?" cried Ned.

"Everything going good! I don't like this business, but now I'm in it I'm going to stick. Put me down a little lower," answered the young inventor.

"All right. I say Tom, look over there."

"Where?"

"By that lightning-struck gum tree. See those

two men, and some sort of a machine they've got stuck up on stilts? See it?"

"Sure. Those are the two Englishmen—my rivals! They're taking pictures, too!"

And then, with a crash and roar, with wild shouts and yells, with volley after volley of fire-arms, clouds of smoke and flights of arrows and spears, the native battle was in full swing, while the young inventor, sailing above it in his air-ship, reeled off view after view of the strange sight.

CHAPTER XIX

A HEAVY LOSS

"Bless my battle axe, but this is awful!" cried Mr. Damon.

"War is always a fearful thing," spoke Mr. Nestor. "But this is not as bad as if the natives fought with modern weapons. See! most of them are fighting with clubs, and their fists. They don't seem to hurt each other very much."

"That's so," agreed Mr. Damon. The two gentlemen were in the main cabin, looking down on the fight below them, while Tom, with Ned to help him change the reels of films, as they became filled with pictures, attended to the camera. Koku was steering the craft, as he had readily learned how to manage it.

"Are those Englishmen taking pictures yet?" asked Tom, too busy to turn his head, and look for himself.

"Yes, they're still at," replied Ned. "But they seem to be having trouble with their machine," he added as he saw one of the men leave the apparatus, and run hurriedly back to where they had made a temporary camp.

"I guess it's an old-fashioned kind," commented Tom. "Say, this is getting fierce!" he cried, as the natives got in closer contact with each other. It was now a hand-to-hand battle.

"I should say so!" yelled Ned. "It's a wonder those Engilshmen aren't afraid to be down on the same level with the black fighters."

"Oh, a white person is considered almost sacred by the natives here, so the missionaries told me," said Tom. "A black man would never think of raising his hand to one, and the Englishmen probably know this. They're safe enough. In fact I'm thinking of soon going down myself, and getting some views from the ground."

"Bless my gizzard, Tom!" cried Mr. Damon. "Don't do it!"

"Yes, I think I will. Why, it's safe enough. Besides, if they attack us we have the electric rifles. Ned, you tell Koku to get the guns out, to have in readiness, and then you put the ship down. I'll take a chance."

"Jove! You've been doing nothing but take chances since we came on this trip!" exclaimed Ned, admiringly. "All right! Here we go," and he went to relieve Koku at the wheel, while the giant, grinning cheerfully at the prospect of taking part in the fight himself, got out the rifles, including his own.

Meanwhile the native battle went on fiercely. Many on both sides fell, and not a few ran away, when they got the chance, their companions yelling at them, evidently trying to shame them into coming back.

As the airship landed, Mr. Damon, Mr. Nestor, Ned and Koku stood ready with the deadly electric rifles, in case an attack should be made on them. But the fighting natives paid no more attention to our friends than they did to the two Englishmen. The latter moved their clumsy camera from place to place, in order to get various views of the fighting.

"This is the best yet!" cried Tom, as, after a lull in the fight, when the two opposing armies had drawn a little apart, they came together again more desperately than before. "I hope the pictures are being recorded all right. I have to go at this thing pretty much in the dark. Say, look at the beggars fight!" he finished.

But a battle, even between uncivilized blacks, cannot go on for very long at a time. Many had fallen, some being quite severely injured it seemed, being carried off by their friends. Then, with a sudden rush, the side which, as our friends learned later, had been robbed of their cattle, made a fierce attack, overwhelming their enemies, and compelling them to retreat. Across the open plain the vanquished army fled, with the others after them. Tom, meanwhile, taking pictures as fast as he could.

"This ends it!" he remarked to Ned, when the warriors were too far away to make any more good views. "Now we can take a rest."

"The Englishmen gave up some time ago," said his chum, motioning to the two men who were taking their machine off the tripod.

"Guess their films gave out," spoke Tom. "Well, you see it didn't do any harm to come down, and I got some better views here."

"Here they come back!" exclaimed Ned, as a horde of the black fellows emerged from the jungle, and came on over the plain.

"Hear 'em sing!" commented Tom, as the sound of a rude chant came to their ears. "They must be the winners all right."

"I guess so," agreed Ned. "But what about staying here now? Maybe they won't be so friendly to us when they haven't any fighting to occupy their minds."

"Don't worry," advised Tom. "They won't bother us."

And the blacks did not. They were caring for their wounded, who had not already been taken from the field, and they paid no attention to our friends, save to look curiously at the airship.

"Bless my newspaper!" cried Mr. Damon, with an air of relief. "I'm glad that's over, and we didn't have to use the electric rifles, after all."

"Here come the Englishmen to pay us a visit," spoke Ned a little later, as they sat about the cabin of the *Flyer*. The two rival picture men soon climbed on deck.

"Beg pardon," said the taller of the two, addressing our hero, "but could you lend us a roll of film? Ours are all used up, and we want to get some more pictures before going back to our main camp."

"I'm sorry," replied Tom, "but I use a special size, and it fits no camera but my own."

"Ah! might we see your camera?" asked the other Englishman. "That is, see how it works?"

"I don't like to be disobliging," was Tom's answer, "but it is not yet patented and—— well——" he hesitated.

"Oh, I see!" sneered the taller visitor. "You're afraid we might steal some of your ideas. Hum! Come on Montgomery," and, swinging on his heels, with a military air, he hurried away, followed by his companion.

"They don't like that, but I can't help it," remarked Tom to his friends a little later. "I can't afford to take any chances."

"No, you did just right," said Mr. Nestor. "Those men may be all right, but from the fact that they are in the picture taking business I'd be suspicious of them."

"Well, what's next on the programme?" asked Ned as Tom put his camera away.

"Oh, I think we'll stay here over night," was our hero's reply. "It's a nice location, and the gas machine needs cleaning. We can do it here, and maybe I can get some more pictures."

They were busy the rest of the day on the gas generator, but the main body of natives did not come back, and the Englishmen seemed to have disappeared.

Everyone slept soundly that night. So soundly, in fact, that the sun was very high when Koku was the first to awaken, His head felt strangely dizzy, and he wondered at a queer smell in the room he had to himself.

"Nobody up yet," he exclaimed in surprise, as he staggered into the main cabin. There, too, was the strange, sweetish, sickly smell. "Mr. Tom, where you be? Time to get up!" the giant called to his master, as he went in, and gently shook the young inventor by the shoulder.

"Eh? What's that? What's the matter?" began Tom, and then he suddenly sat up. "Oh, my head!" he exclaimed, putting his hands to his aching temples.

"And that queer smell!" added Ned, who was also awake now.

"Bless my talcum powder!" cried Mr. Damon. "I have a splitting headache."

"Hum! Chloroform, if I'm any judge!" called Mr. Nestor from his berth.

"Chloroform!" cried Tom, staggering to his feet. "I wonder——" He did not finish his sentence, but made his way to the room where his camera was kept. "It's gone!" he cried. "We have been chloroformed in the night, and some one has taken my Wizard Camera."

CHAPTER XX

AFTER THE ENGLISHMEN

"THE camera gone!" gasped Ned.

"Did they chloroform us?" exclaimed Mr. Damon. "Bless my——" but for one of the few times in his life, he did not know what to bless.

"Get all the fresh air you can," hastily advised Mr. Nestor. "Koku, open all the doors and windows," for, though it was hot during the day in the jungle, the nights were cool, and the airship was generally closed up. With the inrush of the fresh air every one soon felt better.

"Is anything else gone?" asked Ned, as he followed Tom into the camera room.

"Yes, several rolls of unexposed films. Oh, if only they haven't got too much of a start! I'll get it away from them!" declared Tom with energy.

"From who? Who took it?" asked Ned.

"Those Englishmen, of course! Who else? I believe they are in the pay of Turbot and Eckert. Their taking pictures was only a bluff! They got on my trail and stuck to it. The delays we had, gave them a chance to catch up to us. They came over to the airship, to pretend to borrow films, just to get a look at the place, and size it up, so they could chloroform us, and get the camera."

"I believe you're right," declared Mr. Nestor. "We must get after those scoundrels as quickly as possible!"

"Bless my shoulder braces!" cried Mr. Damon. "How do you imagine they worked that trick on us?"

"Easily enough," was Mr. Nestor's opinion. "We were all dead tired last night, and slept like tops. They watched their chance, sneaked up, and got in. After that it was no hard matter to chloroform each one of us in turn, and they had the ship to themselves. They looked around, found the camera, and made off with it."

"Well, I'm going to get right after them!" cried Tom. "Ned, start the motor. I'll steer for a while."

"Hold on! Wait a minute," suggested Mr. Nestor. "I wouldn't go off in the ship just yet, Tom."

"Why not?"

"Because you don't know which way to go. We must find out which trail the Englishmen took. They have African porters with them, and those porters doubtless know some of the blacks around here. We must inquire of the natives which way the porters went, in carrying the goods of our rivals, for those Englishmen would not abandon camp without taking their baggage with them."

"That's so," admitted the young inventor. "That will be the best plan. Once I find which way they have gone I can easily overtake them in the airship. And when I find 'em——" Tom paused significantly.

"Me help you fix 'em!" cried Koku, clenching his big fist.

"They will probably figure it out that you will take after them," said Mr. Nestor, "but they may not count on you doing it in the *Flyer*, and so they may not try to hide. It isn't going to be an easy matter to pick a small party out of the jungle though, Tom."

"Well, I've done more difficult things in my airships," spoke our hero. "I'll fly low, and use the glass. I guess we can pick out their crowd of porters, though they won't have many. Oh, my camera! I hope they won't damage it."

"They won't," was Ned's opinion. "It's too valuable. They want it to take pictures with, themselves."

"Maybe. I hope they don't open it, and see how it's made. And I'm glad I thought to hide the picture films I've taken so far. They didn't get those away from us, only some of the blank ones," and Tom looked again in a secret closet, where he kept the battle-films, and the others, in the dark, to prevent them from being light-struck, by any possible chance.

"Well, if we're going to make some inquiries, let's do it," suggested Mr. Nestor. "I think I see some of the Africans over there. They have made a temporary camp, it seems, to attend to some of their wounded."

"Do you think we can make them understand what we want?" asked Ned. "I don't believe they speak English."

"Oh these blacks have been trading with white men," said Tom, "for they have 'trader's' guns, built to look at, and not to shoot very well. I fancy we can make ourselves understood. If not, we can use signs."

Leaving Koku and Mr. Damon to guard the airship, Tom, Ned and Mr. Nestor went to the African camp. There was a large party of men there, and they seemed friendly enough. Proba-bly winning the battle the day before had put them in good humor, even though many of them were hurt.

To Tom's delight he found one native who could speak a little English, and of him they made inquiries as to what direction the Englishmen had taken. The black talked for a while among his fellows, and then reported to our friends that, late in the night, one of the porters, hired by Montgomery and Kenneth, had come to camp to bid a brother good-bye. This porter had said that his masters were in a hurry to get away, and had started west.

"That's it!" cried Mr. Nestor. "They're going to get somewhere so they can make their way to the coast. They want to get out of Africa as fast as they can."

"And I'm going to get after 'em as fast as *I* can!" cried Tom grimly. "Come on!"

They hurried back to the airship, finding Koku and Mr. Damon peacefully engaged in talk, no one having disturbed them.

"Start the motor, Ned!" called his chum. "We'll see what luck we have!"

Up into the air went the *Flyer,* her great propellers revolving rapidly. Over the jungle she shot, and then, when he found that everything was working well, and that the cleaned gas generator was operating as good as when it was new, the young inventor slowed up, and brought the craft down to a lower level.

"For we don't want to run past these fellows, or shoot over their heads in our hurry," Tom explained. "Ned, get out the binoculars. They're easier to handle than the telescope. Then go up forward, and keep a sharp lookout. There is something like a jungle trail below us, and it looks to be the only one around here. They probably took that." Soon after leaving the place where they had camped after the battle, Tom had seen a rude path through the forest, and had followed that lead.

On sped the *Flyer,* after the two Englishmen, while Tom thought regretfully of his stolen camera.

CHAPTER XXI

THE JUNGLE FIRE

"WELL, Tom, I don't seem to see anything of them," remarked Ned that afternoon, as he sat in the bow of the air craft, gazing from time to time through the powerful glasses.

"No, and I can't understand it, either," responded the young inventor, who had come forward to relieve his chum. "They didn't have much the start of us, and they'll have to travel very slowly. It isn't as if they could hop on a train; and, even if they did, I could overtake them in a short time. But they have to travel on foot through the jungle, and can't have gone far."

"Maybe they have bullock carts," suggested Mr. Damon.

"The trail isn't wide enough for that," declared Tom. "We've come quite a distance now, even if we have been running at low speed, and we haven't seen even a black man on the trail," and he motioned to the rude path below them.

"They may have taken a boat and slipped down that river we crossed a little while ago," suggested Ned.

"That's so!" cried Tom. "Why didn't I think of it? Say! I'm going to turn back."

"Turn back?"

"Yes, and go up and down the stream a way. We have time, for we can easily run at top speed on the return trip. Then, if we don't see anything of them on the water, we'll pick up the trail again. Put her around, Ned, and I'll take the glasses for a while."

The *Flyer* was soon shooting back over the same trail our friends had covered, and, as Ned set the propellers going at top speed, they were quickly hovering over a broad, but shallow river, which cut through the jungle.

"Try it down stream first," suggested Tom, who was peering through the binoculars. "They'd be most likely to go down, as it would be easier."

Along over the stream swept the airship, covering several miles.

"There's a boat!" suddenly exclaimed Mr. Nestor, pointing to a native canoe below them.

"Bless my paddle wheel! So it is!" cried Mr. Damon. "I believe it's them, Tom!"

"No, there are only natives in that craft," answered the young inventor a moment later, as he brought the binoculars into focus. "I wish it *was* them, though."

A few more miles were covered down stream, and then Tom tried the opposite direction. But all to no purpose. A number of boats were seen, and several rafts, but they had no white men on them.

"Maybe the Englishmen disguised themselves like natives, Tom," suggested Ned.

Our hero shook his head.

"I could see everything in the boats, through these powerful glasses," he replied, "and there was nothing like my camera. "I'd know that a mile off. No, they didn't take to this stream, though they probably crossed it. We'll have to keep on the way we were going. It will soon be night, and we'll have to camp. Then we'll take up the search to-morrow."

It was just getting dusk, and Tom was looking about for a good place to land in the jungle, when Ned, who was standing in the bow, cried:

"I say, Tom, here's a native village just ahead. There's a good place to stop, and we can stay there over night."

"Good!" exclaimed Tom. "And, what's more, we can make some inquiries as to whether or not the Englishmen have passed here. This is great! Maybe we'll come out all right, after all.

They can't travel at night—or at least I don't believe they will—and if they have passed this village we can catch them to-morrow. We'll go down."

They were now over the native town, which was in a natural clearing in the jungle. The natives had by this time caught sight of the big airship over them, and were running about in terror. There was not a man, woman or child in sight when the *Flyer* came down, for the inhabitants had all fled in fright.

"Not much of a chance to make inquiries of these folks," said Mr. Nestor.

"Oh, they'll come back," predicted Tom. "They are naturally curious, and when they see that the thing isn't going to blow up, they'll gather around. I've seen the same thing happen before."

Tom proved a true prophet. In a little while some of the men began straggling back, when they saw our friends walking about the airship, as it rested on the ground. Then came the children, and then the women, until the whole population was gathered about the airship, staring at it wonderingly. Tom made signs of friendship, and was lucky enough to find a native who knew a few French words. Tom was not much of a French scholar, but he could frame a question as to the Englishmen.

"*Oui!*" exclaimed the native, when he understood. Then he rattled off something, which Tom, after having it repeated, and making signs to the man to make sure he understood, said meant that the Englishmen had passed through the village that morning.

"We're on the right trail!" cried the young inventor. "They're only a day's travel ahead of us. We'll catch them to-morrow, and get my camera back."

The natives soon lost all fear of the airship, and some of the chief men even consented to come aboard. Tom gave them a few trifles for presents, and won their friendship to such an extent that a great feast was hastily gotten up in honor of the travelers. Big fires were lighted, and fowls by the score were roasted.

"Say, I'm glad we struck this place!" exclaimed Ned, as he sat on the ground with the others, eating roast fowl. "This is all to the chicken salad!"

"Things are coming our way at last," remarked Tom. "We'll start the first thing in the morning. I wish I had my camera now. I'd take a picture of this scene. Dad would enjoy it, and so would Mrs. Baggert. Oh, I almost wish I was home again. But if I get my camera I've got a lot more work ahead of me."

"What kind?" asked Ned.

"I don't know. I'm to stop in Paris for the next instructions from Mr. Period. He is keeping in touch with the big happenings of the world, and he may send us to Japan, to get some earthquake pictures."

The night was quiet after the feast, and in the morning Tom and his friends sailed off in their airship, leaving behind the wondering and pleased natives, for our hero handed out more presents, of small value to him, but yet such things as the blacks prized highly.

Once more they were flying over the trail, and they put on more speed now, for they were fairly sure that the men they sought were ahead of them about a day's travel. This meant perhaps twenty miles, and Tom figured that he could cover fifteen in a hurry, and then go over the remaining five slowly, so as not to miss his quarry.

"Say, don't you smell something?" asked Ned a little later, when the airship had been slowed down. "Something like smoke?"

"Humph! I believe I do get an odor of something burning," admitted Tom, sniffing the atmosphere.

"Bless my pocket book!" exclaimed Mr.

Damon, "look down there, boys!" He pointed
below, and, to the surprise of the lads, and no
less of himself, he saw many animals hurrying
back along the jungle trail.

There were scores of deer, leaping along, here
and there a tawny lion, and one or two tigers.
Off to one side a rhinoceros crashed his way
through the tangle, and occasionally an elephant
was seen.

"That's queer," cried Ned. "And they're not
paying any attention to each other, either."

"Something is happening," was Mr. Nestor's
opinion. "Those animals are running away from
something."

"Maybe it's an elephant drive," spoke Tom.
"I think——"

But he did not finish. The smell of smoke
suddenly became stronger, and, a moment later,
as the airship rose higher, in response to a change
in the angle of the deflecting rudder, which Ned
shifted, all on board saw a great volume of black
smoke rolling toward the sky.

"A jungle fire!" cried Tom. "The jungle is
burning! That's why the animals are running
back this way."

"We'd better not go on!" shouted Ned, choking a bit, as the smoke rolled nearer.

"No, we've got to turn back!" decided Tom.

"Say, this will stop the Englishmen! They can't go on. We'll go back to the village we left, and wait for them. They're trapped!" And then he added soberly: "I hope my camera doesn't get burnt up!"

CHAPTER XXII

A DANGEROUS COMMISSION

"Look at that smoke!" yelled Ned, as he sent the airship about in a great circle on the backward trail.

"And there's plenty of blaze, too," added Tom. "See the flames eating away! This stuff is as dry as tinder for there hasn't been any rain for months."

"Much hot!" was the comment of the giant, when he felt the warm wind of the fire.

"Bless my fountain pen!" gasped Mr. Damon, as he looked down into the jungle. "See all those animals!"

The trail was now thick with deer, and many small beasts, the names of which Tom did not know. On either side could be heard larger brutes, crashing their way forward to escape the fire behind them.

"Oh, if you only had your camera now!" cried Ned. "You could get a wonderful picture, Tom."

"What's the use of wishing for it. Those Englishmen have it, and——"

"Maybe they're using it!" interrupted Ned.

"No, I don't think they would know how to work it. Do you see anything of them, Ned?"

"Not a sight. But they'll surely have to come back, just as you said, unless they got ahead of the fire. They can't go on, and it would be madness to get off the trail in a jungle like this."

"I don't believe they could have gotten ahead of the fire," spoke Tom. "They couldn't travel fast enough for that, and see how broad the blaze is."

They were now higher up, well out of the heat and smoke of the conflagration, and they could see that it extended for many miles along the trail, and for a mile or so on either side of it.

"We're far enough in advance, now, to go down a bit, I guess," said Tom, a little later. "I want to get a good view of the path, and I can't do that from up here. I have an idea that——"

Tom did not finish, for as the airship approached nearer the ground, he caught up a pair of binoculars, and focussed them on something on the trail below.

"What is it?" cried Ned, startled by something in his chum's manner.

"It's them! The Englishmen!" cried Tom. "See, they are racing back along the trail. Their porters have deserted them. But they have my camera! I can see it! I'm going down, and get it! Ned, stand by the wheel, and make a quick landing. Then we'll go up again!"

Tom handed the glasses to his chum, and Ned quickly verified the young inventor's statement. There were the two rascally Englishmen. The fire was still some distance in the rear, but was coming on rapidly. There were no animals to be seen, for they had probably gone off on a side trail, or had slunk deeper into the jungle. Above the distant roar of the blaze sounded the throb of the airship's motor. The Englishmen heard it, and looked up. Then, suddenly, they motioned to Tom to descend.

"That's what I'm going to do," he said aloud, but of course they could not hear him.

"They're waiting for us!" cried Ned. "I wonder why?" for the rascals had come to a halt, setting down the packs they carried on the trail. One of the things they had was undoubtedly Tom's camera.

"They probably want us to save their lives," said Tom. "They know they can't out-run this fire. They've given up! We have them now!"

"Are you going to save them?" asked Mr. Damon.

"Of course. I wouldn't let my worst enemy run the chances of danger in that terrible blaze.

I'd save them even if they had smashed my camera. I'll go down, and get them, and take them back to the native village, but that's as far as I *will* carry them. They'll have to get away as best they can, after that."

It was the work of but a few minutes to lower the airship to the trail. Fortunately it widened a bit at this point, or Tom could never have gotten his craft down through the trees.

"Hand up that camera!" ordered our hero curtly, when he had stopped near the Englishmen.

"Yes, my dear chap," spoke the tall Britisher, "but will you oblige us, by taking us——"

"Hand up the camera first!" sharply ordered Tom again.

They passed it to him.

"I know we treated you beastly mean," went on Kenneth, "but, my dear chap——"

"Get aboard," was all Tom said, and when the rascals, with fearful glances back into the burning jungle, did so, our hero sent his craft high into the air again.

"Where are you taking us, my dear chap?" asked the tall rascal.

"Don't 'dear chap' me!" retorted Tom. "I don't want to talk to you. I'm going to drop you at the native village."

"But that will burn!" cried the Englishman.

"The wind is changing," was our hero's answer. "The fire won't get to the village. You'll be safe. Have you damaged my camera?" he asked as he began to examine it, while Ned managed the ship.

"No, my dear chap. You mustn't think too hard of us. We were both down on our luck, and a chap offered us a big sum to get on your trail, and secure the camera. He said you had filched it from him, and that he had a right to it. Understand, we wouldn't have taken it had we known——"

"Don't talk to me!" interrupted Tom, as he saw that his apparatus had not been damaged. "The man who hired you was a rascal—that's all I'll say. Put on a little more speed, Ned. I want to get rid of these 'dear chaps' and take some pictures of the jungle fire."

As Tom had said, the wind had changed, and was blowing the flames away off to one side, so that the native village would be in no danger. It was soon reached, and the Africans were surprised to see Tom's airship back again. But he did not stay long, descending only to let the Englishmen alight. They pleaded to be taken to the coast, making all sorts of promises, and stating that, had they known that Turbot and Eckert (for whom they admitted they had acted) were not telling the truth, they never would have taken Tom's camera.

"Don't leave us here!" they pleaded.

"I wouldn't have you on board my airship another minute for a fortune!" declared Tom, as he signalled to Ned to start the motor. Then the *Flyer* ascended on high, leaving the plotters and started back for the fire, of which Tom got a series of fine moving pictures.

A week later our friends were in Paris, having made a quick trip, on which little of incident occurred, though Tom managed to get quite a number of good views on the way.

He found a message awaiting him, from Mr. Period.

"Well, where to now?" asked Ned, as his chum read the cablegram.

"Great Scott!" cried our hero. "Talk about hair-raising jobs, this certainly is the limit!"

"Why, what's the matter?"

"I've got to get some moving pictures of a volcano in action," was the answer. "Say, if I'd known what sort of things 'Spotty' wanted, I'd never have consented to take this trip. A volcano in action, and maybe an earthquake on the side! This is certainly going some!"

CHAPTER XXIII

AT THE VOLCANO

"AND you've got to snap-shot a volcano?" remarked Ned to his chum, after a moment of surprised silence. "Any particular one? Is it Vesuvius? If it is we haven't far to go. But how does Mr. Period know that it's going to get into action when we want it to?"

"No, it isn't Vesuvius," replied Tom. "We've got to take another long trip, and we'll have to go by steamer again. The message says that the Arequipa volcano, near the city of the same name, in Peru, has started to 'erupt,' and, according to rumor, it's acting as it did many years ago, just before a big upheaval."

"Bless my Pummice stones!" cried Mr. Damon. "And are you expected to get pictures of it shooting out flames and smoke, Tom?"

"Of course. An inactive volcano wouldn't make much of a moving picture. Well, if we go to Peru, we won't be far from the United States, and we can fly back home in the airship. But we've got to take the *Flyer* apart, and pack up again."

"Will you have time?" asked Mr. Nestor. "Maybe the volcano will get into action before 'you arrive, and the performance will be all over with."

"I think not," spoke Tom, as he again read the cablegram. "Mr. Period says he has advices from Peru to the effect that, on other occasions, it took about a month from the time smoke was first seen coming from the crater, before the fireworks started up. I guess we've got time enough, but we won't waste any."

"And I guess Montgomery and Kenneth won't be there to make trouble for us," put in Ned. "It will be some time before they get away from that African town, I think."

They began work that day on taking the airship apart for transportation to the steamer that was to carry them across the ocean. Tom decided on going to Panama, to get a series of pictures on the work of digging that vast canal. On nquiry he learned that a steamer was soon to sail for Colon, so he took passage for his friends and himself on that, also arranging for the carrying of the parts of his airship.

It was rather hard work to take the *Flyer* apart, but it was finally done, and, in about a week from the time of arriving in Paris, they left that beautiful city. The pictures already taken were forwarded to Mr. Period, with a letter of explanation of Tom's adventures thus far, and an account of how his rivals had acted.

Just before sailing, Tom received another message from his strange employer. The cablegram read:

"Understand our rivals are also going to try for volcano pictures. Can't find out who will represent Turbot and Eckert, but watch out. Be suspicious of strangers."

"That's what I will!" cried Tom. "If they get my camera away from me again, it will be my own fault."

The voyage to Colon was not specially interesting. They ran into a terrific storm, about half way over, and Tom took some pictures from the steamer's bridge, the captain allowing him to do so, but warning him to be careful.

"I'll take Koku up there with me," said the young inventor, "and if a wave tries to wash me overboard he'll grab me."

And it was a good thing that he took this precaution, for, while a wave did not get as high as the bridge, one big, green roller smashed over the bow of the vessel, staggering her so that Tom was tossed against the rail. He would have been seriously hurt, and his camera might have been broken, but for the quickness of the giant.

Koku caught his master, camera and all, in one mighty arm, and with the other clung to a stanchion, holding Tom in safety until the ship was on a level keel once more.

"Thanks, Koku!" gasped Tom. "You always seem to be around when I need you." The giant grinned happily.

The storm blew out in a few days, and, from then on, there was pleasant sailing. When Tom's airship had been reassembled at Colon, it created quite a sensation among the small army of canal workers, and, for their benefit, our hero gave several flying exhibitions.

He then took some of the engineers on a little trip, and in turn, they did him the favor of letting him get moving pictures of parts of the work not usually seen.

"And now for the volcano!" cried Tom one morning, when having shipped to Mr. Period the canal pictures, the *Flyer* was sent aloft, and her nose pointed toward Arequipa. "We've got quite a run before us."

"How long?" asked Ned.

"About two thousand miles. But I'm going to

speed her up to the limit." Tom was as good as his word, and soon the *Flyer* was shooting along at her best rate, reeling off mile after mile, just below the clouds.

It was a wild and desolate region over which the travelers found themselves most of the time, though the scenery was magnificent. They sailed over Quito, that city on the equator, and, a little later, they passed above the Cotopaxi and Chimborazo volcanoes. But neither of them was in action. The Andes Mountains, as you all know, has many volcanoes scattered along the range. Lima was the next large city, and there Tom made a descent to inquire about the burning mountain he was shortly to photograph.

"It will soon be in action," the United States counsel said. "I had a letter from a correspondent near there only yesterday, and he said the people in the town were getting anxious. They are fearing a shower of burning ashes, or that the eruption may be accompanied by an earthquake."

"Good!" cried Tom. "Oh, I don't mean it exactly that way," he hastened to add, as he saw the counsel looking queerly at him. "I meant that I could get pictures of both earthquake and volcano then. I don't wish the poor people any harm."

"Well, you're the first one I ever saw who was

anxious to get next door to a volcano," remarked
the counsel. "Hold on, though, that's not quite
right. I heard yesterday that a couple of young
fellows passed through here on their way to the
same place. Come to think of it, they were moving picture men, also."

"Great Scott!" cried Tom. "Those must be
my rivals, I'll wager. I must get right on the job.
Thanks for the information," and hurrying from
the office he joined his friends on the airship,
and was soon aloft again.

"Look, Tom, what's that?" cried Ned, about
noon the next day when the *Flyer,* according to
their calculations must be nearing the city of Arequipa. "See that black cloud over there. I hope
it isn't a tornado, or a cyclone, or whatever they
call the big wind storms down here."

Tom, and the others, looked to where Ned
pointed. There was a column of dense smoke
hovering in the air, lazily swirling this way and
that. The airship was rapidly approaching it.

"Why that——" began Tom, but before he
could complete the sentence the smoke was blown
violently upward. It became streaked with fire,
and, a moment later, there was the echo of a tremendous explosion.

"The volcano!" cried Tom. "The Arequipa
volcano! We're here just in time, for she's in

eruption now! Come on, Ned, help me get out the camera! Mr. Damon, you and Mr. Nestor manage the airship! Put us as close as you dare! I'm going to get some crackerjack pictures!"

Once more came a great report.

"Bless my toothpick!" gasped Mr. Damon. "This is awful!" And the airship rushed on toward the volcano which could be plainly seen now, belching forth fire, smoke and ashes.

CHAPTER XXIV

THE MOLTEN RIVER

"Whew!" gasped Ned, as he stood beside Tom in the bow of the airship. "What's that choking us, Tom?"

"Sulphur, I guess, and gases from the volcano. The wind blew 'em over this way. They're not dangerous, as long as there is no carbonic acid gas given off, and I don't smell any of that, yet. Say, Ned, it's erupting all right, isn't it?"

"I should say so!" cried his chum.

"Put us a little to one side, Mr. Damon," called Tom to his friend, who was in the pilot house. "I can't get good pictures through so much smoke. "It's clearer off to the left."

"Bless my bath robe!" cried the odd man. "You're as cool about it, Tom, as though you were just in an ordinary race, at an aeroplane meet."

"And why shouldn't I be?" asked our hero with a laugh, as he stopped the mechanism of the camera until he should have a clearer view of the volcano. "There's not much danger up here, but I want to get some views from the level, later, and then——"

"You don't get *me* down there!" interrupted Mr. Nestor, with a grim laugh.

They were now hovering over the volcano, but high enough up so that none of the great stones that were being thrown out could reach them. The column of black smoke, amid which could be seen the gleams of the molten fires in the crater, rolled toward them, and the smell of sulphur became stronger.

But when, in accordance with Tom's suggestion, the airship had been sent over to one side, they were clear of the vapor and the noxious gas. Then, too, a better view could be had of the volcano below them.

"Hold her down!" cried Tom, as he got in a good position, and the propellers were slowed down so that they just overcame the influence of a slight wind. Thus the *Flyer* hovered in the air, while below her the volcano belched forth red-hot rocks, some of them immense in size, and quantities of hot ashes and cinders. Tom had the camera going again now, and there was every prospect of getting a startling and wonderful, as well as rare series of moving pictures.

"Wow! That was a big one!" cried Ned, as

an unusually large mass of rocks was thrown out, and the column of fire and smoke ascended nearly to the hovering craft. A moment later came an explosion, louder than any that had preceeded. "We'd better be going up; hadn't we Tom?" his chum asked.

"A little, yes, but not too far. I want to get as many near views as I can."

"Bless my overshoes!" gasped Mr. Damon, as he heard Tom say that. Then he sent some of the vapor from the generating machine into the gas bag, and the *Flyer* arose slightly.

Ned looked in the direction of the town, but could not see it, on account of the haze. Then he directed his attention to the terrifying sight below him.

"It's a good thing it isn't very near the city," he said to Tom, who was engaged in watching the automatic apparatus of the camera, to see when he would have to put in a fresh film. "It wouldn't take much of this sort of thing to destroy a big city. But I don't see any streams of burning lava, such as they always say come out of a volcano."

"It isn't time for that yet," replied Tom. "The lava comes out last, after the top layer of stones and ashes have been blown out. They are a sort of stopper to the volcano, I guess, like the cork of a bottle, and, when they're out of the way, the red-hot melted rock comes out. Then there's trouble. I want to get pictures of that."

"Well, keep far enough away," advised Mr. Nestor, who had come forward. "Don't take any chances. I guess your rivals won't get here in time to take any pictures, for they can't travel as fast as we did."

"No," agreed the young inventor, "unless some other party of them were here ahead of us. They'll have their own troubles, though, making pictures anything like as good as we're getting."

"There goes another blast!" cried Ned, as a terrific explosion sounded, and a shower of hot stuff was thrown high into the air. "If I lived in Arequipa I'd be moving out about now."

"There isn't much danger I guess, except from showers of burning ashes, and volcanic dust," spoke Mr. Nestor, "and the wind is blowing it away from the town. If it continues this way the people will be saved."

"Unless there is so much of the red-hot lava that it will bury the city," suggested Tom. "I hope that doesn't happen," and he could not repress a shudder as he looked down on the awful scene below him.

After that last explosion the volcano appeared

to subside somewhat, though great clouds of smoke and tongues of fire leaped upward.

"I've got to put in a new reel of film!" suddenly exclaimed Tom. "While I stop the camera, Mr. Damon, I think you and Mr. Nestor might put the airship down to the ground. I want some views on the level."

"What! Go down to earth with this awful volcano spouting fire?" cried Mr. Damon. "Bless my comb and brush!"

"We can get well down the side of the mountain," said Tom. "I won't go into any danger, much less ask any one else to do so, and I certainly don't want my ship damaged. We can land down there," he said, pointing to a spot on the side of the volcanic mountain, that was some distance removed from the mouth of the crater. It won't take me long to get one reel of views, and then I'll come up again."

The two men finally gave in to Tom's argument, that there was comparatively little danger, for they admitted that they could quickly rise up at the first sign of danger, and accordingly the *Flyer* descended. Tom quickly had a fresh reel of film, inserted, and started his camera to working, standing it on a tripod some distance from the airship.

Once more the volcano was "doing its prettiest," as Tom expressed it. He glanced around, as another big explosion took place, to see if any other picture men were on hand, but the terrible mountain seemed deserted, though of course someone might be on the other side.

"What's that?" suddenly cried Ned, looking apprehensively at his chum. At the same time Tom jumped to his feet, for he had been kneeling near the camera.

"Bless my——" began Mr. Damon, but he got no farther, for suddenly the solid ground began to tremble and shake.

"An earthquake!" shouted Mr. Nestor. "Come, Tom! Get back to the ship!" The young inventor and Ned had been the only ones to leave it, as it rested on a spur of the mountain.

As Tom and Ned leaped forward to save the camera which was toppling to one side, there came a great fissure in the side of the volcano, and a stream of molten rock, glowing white with heat, gushed out. It was a veritable river of melted stone, and it was coming straight for the two lads.

"Run! Run!" cried Mr. Nestor. "We have everything ready for a quick flight. "Run, Tom! Ned!"

The lads leaped for the *Flyer,* the molten rock coming nearer and nearer, and then with a cry Koku sprang overboard and made a dash toward his master.

CHAPTER XXV

THE EARTHQUAKE—CONCLUSION

"Here, Mr. Tom. Me carry you an' Ned. You hold picture machine!" cried the giant. "Me run faster."

As he spoke he lifted Ned up under one arm, and caught Tom in the other. For they were but as children to his immense strength. Tom held on to his camera, and, thus laden down, Koku ran as he had never run before, toward the waiting airship.

"Come on! Come on!" shouted Mr. Damon, for he could see what Tom, Ned and Koku could not, that the stream of lava was nearing them rapidly.

"It's hot!" cried Ned, as a wave of warm air fanned his cheek.

"I should say so!" cried Tom. "The volcano is full of red-hot melted stone."

There came a sickening shake of the earth. Koku staggered as he ran on, but he kept his feet, and did not fall. Again came a tremendous explosion, and a shower of fine ashes sifted over the airship, and on Koku and his living burdens.

"This is the worst ever!" gasped Tom. "But I've got some dandy pictures, if we ever get away from here alive to develope them."

"Hurry, Koku! Hurry!" begged Mr. Nestor.

"Bless my shoe laces!" yelled Mr. Damon, who was fairly jumping up and down on the deck of the *Flyer*. "I'll never go near a volcano again!"

Once more the ground shook and trembled, as the earthquake rent it. Several cracks appeared in Koku's path, but he leaped over them with tremendous energy. A moment later he had thrust Tom and Ned over the rail, to the deck, and leaped aboard himself.

"Let her go!" cried Tom. "I'll do the rest of my moving picture work, around volcanoes and earthquakes, from up in the air!"

The *Flyer* shot upward, and scarcely a moment too soon, for, an instant after she left the ground, the stream of hot, burning and bubbling lava rolled beneath her, and those on board could feel the heat of it ascending.

"Say, I'm glad we got out of that when we did," gasped Ned, as he looked down. "You're all right, Koku."

"That no trouble," replied the giant with a cheerful grin. "Me carry four fellows like you," and he stretched out his big arms. Tom had at once set his camera to working again, taking view after view.

It was a terrifying but magnificent sight that our friends beheld, for the earth was trembling and heaving. Great fissures opened in many places. Into some of them streams of lava poured, for now the volcano had opened in several places, and from each crack the melted rocks belched out. The crater, however, was not sending into the air such volumes of smoke and ashes as before, as most of the tremendous energy had passed, or was being used to spout out the lava.

The earthquake was confined to the region right about the volcano, or there might have been a great loss of life in the city. As it was, the damage done was comparatively slight.

Tom continued to take views, some showing the earth as it was twisted and torn, and other different aspects of the crater. Then, as suddenly as the earthquake had begun, it subsided, and the volcano was less active.

"My! I'm glad to see that!" exclaimed Mr. Damon. "I've had about enough of horrors!"

"And I have too," added Tom. "I'm on my last roll of film, and I can't take many more pictures. But I guess I have all Mr. Period needs, and we'll start for home, as soon as I finish the next roll. But I'm going to save that for a night view. That will be a novelty."

The volcano became active again after dark, and presented a magnificent though terrifying aspect. As the airship hovered above it, Tom got some of his best pictures, and then, as the last bit of film slipped along back of the lens, the airship was headed north.

"Now for Shopton!" cried Tom. "Our trip is ended."

"It's too bad you didn't have more film," said Ned. "I thought you had plenty."

"Well, I used more than I counted on, but there are enough pictures as it is."

"Plenty," agreed Mr. Nestor. "I'm sure our company will be very well satisfied with them, Tom. We can't get home any too soon to suit me. I've had enough excitement."

"And we didn't see anything of those other fellows whom we heard about," spoke Mr. Damon, as the big airship flew on.

"No," said Tom. "But I'm not worrying about them."

They made another stop in Lima, on their homeward trip, to renew their supply of gasolene, and there learned that the rival picture men had arrived at the volcano too late to see it in operation. This news came to a relative of one of the two men who lived in Lima.

"Then our views of the earthquake and the smoking mountain will be the *only* ones, and your company can control the rights," said Tom to Mr. Nestor, who agreed with him.

In due time, and without anything out of the ordinary happening the *Flyer* reached Shopton, where Tom found a warm welcome awaiting him, not only from his father, but from a certain young lady, whose name I do not need to mention.

"And so you got everything you went after, didn't you, Tom," exclaimed Mr. Period, a few days later, when he had come from New York to get the remainder of the films.

"Yes, and some things I didn't expect," replied Tom. "There was——"

"Yes! Yes! I know!" interrupted the odd picture man. "It was that jungle fire. That's a magnificent series. None better. And those scoundrels took your camera; eh?"

"Yes. Could you connect them with Turbot and Eckert?" asked Tom.

"No, but I'm sure they were acting for them just the same. I had no legal evidence to act on, however, so I had to let it go. Turbot and Eckert won't be in it when I start selling duplicates of the films you have. And these last ought to be the best of all. I didn't catch that fellow when I raced after him on the dock. He got away, and has steered clear of me since," finished Mr. Period.

"And our rivals didn't secure any views like ours," said Tom.

"I'm glad of it," spoke Mr. Period. "Turbot and Eckert bribed one of my men, and so found out where I was sending messages to you. They even got a copy of my cablegram. But it did them no good."

"Were all the films clear that I sent you?" asked our hero.

"Every one. Couldn't be better. The animal views were particularly fine. You must have had your nerve with you to get some of 'em."

"Oh, Tom always has his nerve," laughed Ned.

"Well, how soon will you be ready to start out again?" asked the picture man, as he packed up the last of the films which Tom gave him. "I'd like to get some views of a Japanese earthquake, and we haven't any polar views. I want some of them, taken as near the North Pole as you can get."

Tom gently shook his head.

"What! You don't mean to say you won't get them for me?" cried Mr. Period. "With that wonderful camera of yours you can get views no one else ever could."

"Then some one else will have to take them," remarked the young inventor. "I'll lend you the camera, and an airship, and you can go yourself, Mr. Period. I'm going to stay home for a while. I did what I set out to do, and that's enough."

"I'm glad you'll stay home, Tom," said his father. "Now perhaps I'll get my gyroscope finished."

"And I, my noiseless airship," went on our hero. "No, Mr. Period, you'll have to excuse me this time. Why don't you go yourself?" he asked. "You would know just what kind of pictures you wanted."

"No, I'm a promoter of the moving picture business, and I sell films, but I don't know how to take them," was the answer. "Besides I.— er—well, I don't exactly care for airships, Tom Swift," he finished with a laugh. "Well, I can't thank you enough for what you did for me, and I've brought you a check to cover your expenses, and pay you as I agreed. All the same I'm sorry you won't start for Japan, or the North Pole."

"Nothing doing," said Tom with a laugh; and Mr. Period departed.

"Have you any idea what you will do next?"

asked Ned, a day or so later, when he and Tom were in the workshop.

"I can't tell until I finish my noiseless airship," was the answer. "Then something may happen."

Something did, as I shall have the pleasure of telling you about in the next volume of this series, to be called, "Tom Swift and His Great Searchlight; or, On the Border for Uncle Sam," and in it will be given an account of a great lantern our hero made, and how he baffled the smugglers with it.

"Oh, Tom, weren't you dreadfully frightened when you saw that burning river of lava coming toward you?" asked Mary Nestor, when the young inventor called on her later and told her some of his adventures. "I should have been scared to death."

"Well, I didn't have time to get scared," answered Tom. "It all happened so quickly, and then, too I was thinking of my camera. Next I knew Koku grabbed me, and it was all over."

"But those wild beasts! Didn't they frighten you, especially when the rhinoceros charged you?"

"If you won't let it get out, I'll make a confession to you," said Tom, lowering his voice. "I *was* scared stiff that time, but don't let Ned know it."

"I won't," promised Mary with a laugh. And now, when Tom is in such pleasant company, we will take leave of him for a while, knowing that, sooner or later, he will be seeking new adventures as exciting as those of the past.

THE END

THE BUNNY BROWN SERIES
By LAURA LEE HOPE
Author of the Popular "Bobbsey Twins" Books

Wrapper and text illustrations drawn by
FLORENCE ENGLAND NOSWORTHY

12mo. DURABLY BOUND. ILLUSTRATED. UNIFORM STYLE OF BINDING

These stories by the author of the "Bobbsey Twins" Books are eagerly welcomed by the little folks from about five to ten years of age. Their eyes fairly dance with delight at the lively doings of inquisitive little Bunny Brown and his cunning, trustful sister Sue.

Bunny was a lively little boy, very inquisitive. When he did anything, Sue followed his leadership. They had many adventures, some comical in the extreme.

BUNNY BROWN AND HIS SISTER SUE

BUNNY BROWN AND HIS SISTER SUE ON GRAND-PA'S FARM

BUNNY BROWN AND HIS SISTER SUE PLAYING CIRCUS

BUNNY BROWN AND HIS SISTER SUE AT CAMP REST-A-WHILE

BUNNY BROWN AND HIS SISTER SUE AT AUNT LU'S CITY HOME

BUNNY BROWN AND HIS SISTER SUE IN THE BIG WOODS

BUNNY BROWN AND HIS SISTER SUE ON AN AUTO TOUR

BUNNY BROWN AND HIS SISTER SUE AND THEIR SHETLAND PONY

BUNNY BROWN AND HIS SISTER SUE GIVING A SHOW

BUNNY BROWN AND HIS SISTER SUE AT CHRIST-MAS TREE COVE

GROSSET & DUNLAP,   PUBLISHERS,   NEW YORK

THE BOBBSEY TWINS BOOKS

For Little Men and Women

By LAURA LEE HOPE

Author of "The Bunny Brown" Series, Etc.

12mo. DURABLY BOUND. ILLUSTRATED. UNIFORM STYLE OF BINDING

Copyright publications which cannot be obtained elsewhere. Books that charm the hearts of the little ones, and of which they never tire.

THE BOBBSEY TWINS

THE BOBBSEY TWINS IN THE COUNTRY

THE BOBBSEY TWINS AT THE SEASHORE

THE BOBBSEY TWINS AT SCHOOL

THE BOBBSEY TWINS AT SNOW LODGE

THE BOBBSEY TWINS ON A HOUSEBOAT

THE BOBBSEY TWINS AT MEADOW BROOK

THE BOBBSEY TWINS AT HOME

THE BOBBSEY TWINS IN A GREAT CITY

THE BOBBSEY TWINS ON BLUEBERRY ISLAND

THE BOBBSEY TWINS ON THE DEEP BLUE SEA

THE BOBBSEY TWINS IN THE GREAT WEST

GROSSET & DUNLAP,   PUBLISHERS,   NEW YORK

THE MOVING PICTURE GIRLS SERIES

By LAURA LEE HOPE

Author of "The Bobbsey Twins Series."

12mo. BOUND IN CLOTH. ILLUSTRATED. UNIFORM STYLE OF BINDING

The adventures of Ruth and Alice DeVere. Their father, a widower, is an actor who has taken up work for the "movies." Both girls wish to aid him in his work and visit various localities to act in all sorts of pictures.

THE MOVING PICTURE GIRLS
Or First Appearance in Photo Dramas.

Having lost his voice, the father of the girls goes into the movies and the girls follow. Tells how many "parlor dramas" are filmed.

THE MOVING PICTURE GIRLS AT OAK FARM
Or Queer Happenings While Taking Rural Plays.

Full of fun in the country, the haps and mishaps of taking film plays, and giving an account of two unusual discoveries.

THE MOVING PICTURE GIRLS SNOWBOUND
Or The Proof on the Film.

A tale of winter adventures in the wilderness, showing how the photo-play actors sometimes suffer.

THE MOVING PICTURE GIRLS UNDER THE PALMS
Or Lost in the Wilds of Florida.

How they went to the land of palms, played many parts in dramas before the camera; were lost, and aided others who were also lost.

THE MOVING PICTURE GIRLS AT ROCKY RANCH
Or Great Days Among the Cowboys.

All who have ever seen moving pictures of the great West will want to know just how they are made. This volume gives every detail and is full of clean fun and excitement.

THE MOVING PICTURE GIRLS AT SEA
Or a Pictured Shipwreck that Became Real.

A thrilling account of the girls' experiences on the water.

THE MOVING PICTURE GIRLS IN WAR PLAYS
Or The Sham Battles at Oak Farm.

The girls play important parts in big battle scenes and have plenty of hard work along with considerable fun.

GROSSET & DUNLAP, PUBLISHERS, NEW YORK

THE GIRLS OF CENTRAL HIGH SERIES

By GERTRUDE W. MORRISON

12mo. BOUND IN CLOTH.   ILLUSTRATED.   UNIFORM STYLE OF BINDING.

Here is a series full of the spirit of high school life of to-day. The girls are real flesh-and-blood characters, and we follow them with interest in school and out. There are many contested matches on track and field, and on the water, as well as doings in the classroom and on the school stage. There is plenty of fun and excitement, all clean, pure and wholesome.

THE GIRLS OF CENTRAL HIGH
Or Rivals for all Honors.
> A stirring tale of high school life, full of fun, with a touch of mystery and a strange initiation.

THE GIRLS OF CENTRAL HIGH ON LAKE LUNA
Or The Crew That Won.
> Telling of water sports and fun galore, and of fine times in camp.

THE GIRLS OF CENTRAL HIGH AT BASKETBALL
Or The Great Gymnasium Mystery.
> Here we have a number of thrilling contests at basketball and in addition, the solving of a mystery which had bothered the high school authorities for a long while.

THE GIRLS OF CENTRAL HIGH ON THE STAGE
Or The Play That Took the Prize.
> How the girls went in for theatricals and how one of them wrote a play which afterward was made over for the professional stage and brought in some much-needed money.

THE GIRLS OF CENTRAL HIGH ON TRACK AND FIELD
Or The Girl Champions of the School League
> This story takes in high school athletics in their most approved and up-to-date fashion. Full of fun and excitement.

THE GIRLS OF CENTRAL HIGH IN CAMP
Or The Old Professor's Secret.
> The girls went camping on Acorn Island and had a delightful time at boating, swimming and picnic parties.

GROSSET & DUNLAP,   PUBLISHERS,   NEW YORK

THE OUTDOOR GIRLS SERIES
By LAURA LEE HOPE
Author of the "Bobbsey Twin Books" and "Bunny Brown"
Series.

12mo. BOUND IN CLOTH.   ILLUSTRATED.   UNIFORM STYLE OF BINDING.

These tales take in the various adventures participated in by several bright, up-to-date girls who love outdoor life. They are clean and wholesome, free from sensationalism, absorbing from the first chapter to the last.

THE OUTDOOR GIRLS OF DEEPDALE
Or Camping and Tramping for Fun and Health.

Telling how the girls organized their Camping and Tramping Club, how they went on a tour, and of various adventures which befell them.

THE OUTDOOR GIRLS AT RAINBOW LAKE
Or Stirring Cruise of the Motor Boat Gem.

One of the girls becomes the proud possessor of a motor boat and invites her club members to take a trip down the river to Rainbow Lake, a beautiful sheet of water lying between the mountains.

THE OUTDOOR GIRLS IN A MOTOR CAR
Or The Haunted Mansion of Shadow Valley.

One of the girls has learned to run a big motor car, and she invites the club to go on a tour to visit some distant relatives. On the way they stop at a deserted mansion and make a surprising discovery.

THE OUTDOOR GIRLS IN A WINTER CAMP
Or Glorious Days on Skates and Ice Boats.

In this story, the scene is shifted to a winter season. The girls have some jolly times skating and ice boating, and visit a hunters' camp in the big woods.

THE OUTDOOR GIRLS IN FLORIDA.
Or Wintering in the Sunny South.

The parents of one of the girls have bought an orange grove in Florida, and her companions are invited to visit the place. They take a trip into the interior, where several unusual things happen.

THE OUTDOOR GIRLS AT OCEAN VIEW
Or The Box that Was Found in the Sand.

The girls have great fun and solve a mystery while on an outing along the New England coast.

THE OUTDOOR GIRLS ON PINE ISLAND
Or A Cave and What it Contained.

A bright, healthful story, full of good times at a bungalow camp on Pine Island.

GROSSET & DUNLAP,   PUBLISHERS,   NEW YORK

CHARMING BOOKS FOR GIRLS

WHEN PATTY WENT TO COLLEGE, By Jean Webster.

Illustrated by C. D. Williams.

One of the best stories of life in a girl's college that has ever been written. It is bright, whimsical and entertaining, lifelike, laughable and thoroughly human.

JUST PATTY, By Jean Webster.

Illustrated by C. M. Relyea.

Patty is full of the joy of living, fun-loving, given to ingenious mischief for its own sake, with a disregard for pretty convention which is an unfailing source of joy to her fellows.

THE POOR LITTLE RICH GIRL, By Eleanor Gates.

With four full page illustrations.

This story relates the experience of one of those unfortunate children whose early days are passed in the companionship of a governess, seldom seeing either parent, and famishing for natural love and tenderness. A charming play as dramatized by the author.

REBECCA OF SUNNYBROOK FARM,   By Kate Douglas Wiggin.

One of the most beautiful studies of childhood—Rebecca's artistic, unusual and quaintly charming qualities stand out midst a circle of austere New Englanders. The stage version is making a phenominal dramatic record.

NEW CHRONICLES OF REBECCA, By Kate Douglas Wiggin.

Illustrated by F. C. Yohn.

Additional episodes in the girlhood of this delightful heroine that carry Rebecca through various stages to her eighteenth birthday.

REBECCA MARY, By Annie Hamilton Donnell.

Illustrated by Elizabeth Shippen Green.

This author possesses the rare gift of portraying all the grotesque little joys and sorrows and scruples of this very small girl with a pathos that is peculiarly genuine and appealing.

EMMY LOU: Her Book and Heart, By George Madden Martin.

Illustrated by Charles Louis Hinton.

Emmy Lou is irresistibly lovable, because she is so absolutely real. She is just a bewitchingly innocent, hugable little maid. The book is wonderfully human.